HOUSE
OF
BONDAGE
BY
ERNEST
COLE

With
Thomas Flaherty

Introduction
by
Joseph Lelyveld

A Ridge Press Book | *Random House* | *New York*

*This book is dedicated to
the memory of my dear Dad, to Struan Robertson,
and to my brethren in bondage.*

Editor-in-Chief: Jerry Mason
Editor: Adolph Suehsdorf
Art Director: Albert Squillace
Art Associate: Allan Mogel
Art Associate: David Namias
Associate Editor: Ruth Birnkrant
Associate Editor: Moira Duggan
Associate Editor: Frances Foley
Art Production: Doris Mullane

CONTENTS

"ONE OF THE LEAST-KNOWN COUNTRIES IN THE WORLD"

By Joseph Lelyveld

Joseph Lelyveld became a friend of Ernest Cole while reporting from South Africa for the New York Times. He was forced out in 1966, when the South African Government refused to renew his alien resident's permit. He currently covers India and Pakistan for the Times.

A white in South Africa who has some need or, less likely, wish to enter an area where black people live must first apply to his local Department of Non-European Affairs for a permit. If the permit is granted, he will find it carries a warning: *"Any person entering any location, Bantu village or Bantu hostel does so at his own risk."* In one sense the warning is superfluous:

It is no secret that the South African Government takes no responsibility for contacts between the races. But the risk needs more spelling out than it gets on the official form. Does a black man go home to his township "at his own risk," or is a "person" white by definition? Risk of what? Assault by black men? The Government insists there is only harmony between the races in this lovely, heartbreaking, violent land. Could loot or hate tempt those young men in the townships with the impassive faces and hard, possibly threatening eyes to violate that harmony by attacking unprotected white visitors? Undoubtedly they could, if unprotected white visitors weren't so very rare. As things stand, such attacks almost never happen. They happen more often outside the townships, but racial separation—itself a form

of white violence—helps insure that the victims of most black violence in South Africa are black: the ultimate achievement, perhaps, of the experiment in human non-relations known as *apartheid.*

For a white South African the real risk of entering a township is something more terrible, in a way even more violent than the remote chance that he may be assaulted. The possibility is at least equally remote, but seeing black South Africans in their sprawling encampments could, just possibly, raise one or two questions about the set of principles that decrees this lopsided form of social organization. The terrible risk is that from an unaccustomed perspective—a random glance through a window or into a yard— the white man might see something that would bring home to him the heavy odds against which black men in his country must struggle to lead decent lives.

That is what Joyce called an epiphany: It is an essential, if less-than-everyday, part of the South African experience. One young Afrikaner told me about his instantaneous conversion from the doctrines of the ruling Nationalist Party to outright liberalism. It happened when an elderly African in an office where he was working part-time asked him if he had any old underwear to spare. "He looked middle class," the young man recalled, "a typical Afrikaans church elder if you changed the color of his skin. It was a trivial incident but I resolved then and there to break off any association I had with *apartheid.*"

More likely that will not happen. More likely the white South African visiting the townships will look at the endless rows of small brick bungalows and concoct for himself some assurance of how happy and grateful the black people inside must be to him and his kind for the roofs over their heads. But he runs the risk, which is why there are few applications for permits and even fewer permits. Most black townships are not even indicated on the ordinary road maps available at Esso or Mobil service stations; no highways cut through them. The newest among them are often unbelievably remote, remoteness being precisely the quality white officials think a black township most needs to be successful. Most white South Africans, in fact, can go for months with-out seeing a black township, a lifetime without entering one. In their solipsistic world, the townships do not exist. "We know the Bantu," most of them will say. But there are few whites, with the exception of Government officials and policemen, who have been where Ernest Cole's camera has been. His South Africa—the South Africa, after all, of most South Africans—is one of the least-known countries in the world.

Suppose, nonetheless, that you are white and have a permit to enter Soweto, Johannesburg's black annex, which, with a population of more than five hundred thousand, is the largest human settlement in the land. There is no bus or train you can take; public transport for whites doesn't stop there. A taxi is out of the question, for you would have to arrange a permit for its white driver. So you drive yourself, finding the un-marked route through the industrial section that fills the southern part of Johannesburg. Only two roads lead in and out of Soweto. The road that goes to the part of the township nearest the center of the city, seven miles distant, runs along a barrier of huge slime dams from the gold mines, then dips under a railway trestle. On the other side of the tracks the faces on the billboards that tip back in enjoyment of Castle Lager Beer suddenly become black. During the rainy season, however, this road is impassable. A small lake forms under the trestle and the long way around becomes the only way into the townships, a slender thread of asphalt connecting the largest black settlement in the country to the largest white settlement.

Soweto is not a Zulu or Xhosa word standing for something like Harmony or the name of some great black leader. It is simply an amalgam of the words South Western Townships—an appropriate bureaucratic designation for this realization of the relentless bureaucratic idea that whites and blacks must live apart. Officially the Government considers Soweto a temporarily unavoidable social aberration in what has now been declared a "white area." Eventually—or so the theory of *apartheid,* at its most preposterous, holds—the entire black urban population will melt back into tribal reserves. Thus, when community leaders in

Soweto meekly requested the right to own their own homes, a cabinet minister replied: "If we allow freehold rights in Soweto, that would be the anchor for Africans to settle permanently in our midst. That is against Government policy."

There are two ways for outsiders to see the townships. One is in the company of proprietary white officials who run standardized tours through the state-run beer halls and breweries, the shops, schools, and selected middle-class residences, explaining along the way how each of these establishments embodies the plenitude of life enjoyed by the black man in South Africa. The other way, which should be easier and more natural but becomes increasingly difficult to manage as the *apartheid* era advances, is in the company of a black resident willing to take the chance of being seen with an outsider. He won't show off Government buildings, which means he will have little to show off: Nearly all buildings in the townships, including the houses, belong to the Government. Instead, he will lead the visitor out of view to someone's parlor or backyard where beer and brandy flow as freely as in a tavern. It doesn't take long to catch on that the similarity is more than passing. The state raises much of the money with which it runs the townships—and, thus, holds down white taxes—by brewing the concoction known as Bantu beer and operating all drinking establishments where black men can legally imbibe. These establishments are big and well-lit, like gymnasiums. Police informers are staked out in them as a matter of course and women are excluded. So most Africans prefer the illegal speakeasies known as shebeens, which operate out of parlors and backyards. These are rarely free of informers; in fact, the police, white as well as black, drop by regularly to collect their rake-off. But here the Bantu beer is spiked to give it a higher alcohol content and there is never any shortage of women.

The talk at the shebeens is ironic and careful, habitually inexplicit. Politics is out. An African friend of mine told me that he could always spot the informers. "They are the people," he said, "who try to strike up a conversation about the A.N.C. or the P.A.C. [The African National Congress and the Pan-Africanist Congress, the outlawed black-nationalist movements.] No man would do that to a friend. It's too dangerous."

Only once did I make any attempt to steer the talk towards politics in a shebeen. It was election day for white South Africa and I wanted to sample the black reaction to this spectacle of the chosen exercising their free choice. The reaction was predictably roundabout and sardonic. "What were you doing at that polling station this morning?" a man who said he was an undertaker asked a friend.

"Voting, of course," the friend replied, taking up the undertaker's morose joke.

"Who for?"

"Well," said the friend, "that's between my conscience and myself, but if you really must know, the candidate's name was Hendrik Verwoerd—he's my man."

The banter and bitter laughter continued, but there was one man who wasn't joining in. "Look," he said at last, his patience giving way, "can't we talk about something else? This subject makes me sick." His feeling was immediately respected. The talk turned to Cassius Clay and why he hadn't knocked out George Chuvalo, then meandered back to the second Louis-Schmeling fight, which is often mentioned in the townships as an early proof of the black man's inherent equality. "That's better," said the man who didn't want to talk about the white election, able at least to enjoy his beer again.

In a few moments we had ranged across the whole burned-out landscape of African political discourse in South Africa today, for between irony and silence there is nothing but a tearing sense of helplessness. Helplessness, not hopelessness: Every black man in South Africa has the ultimate consolation of knowing that time is on his side; sheer numbers make him part of an inevitability. According to demographers, thirty-six million of the forty-two million people who will be living in South Africa in the year 2000 will be non-white. But for the present the black man finds himself trapped in someone else's dream, able only to wait passively for the dreamer to wake or be wakened. He can savor the absurdity of his position but cannot step outside it. His sense of inevitability and his sense of reality

9

give him a great human advantage; at least he knows the score. But as he makes his way through the white world—eighty-six per cent of the South African land is officially proclaimed "white"—these prove no compensation for his sense of futility. His day will come in time, but that passing time is his life. Probably, he knows, it will come too late.

White South Africans can tell you, of course, how they would feel if someone put them in the underdog position in which they have frozen the Africans. But they cannot believe the Africans are capable of such feelings. "Man, don't feel sorry for them," you are always told. "They're happier than you and I. They only live for the moment." There is condescension and envy and a germ of truth in this racial stereotype. Many white South Africans seem too anxiety-ridden to be capable of much happiness, while living for the moment is the only kind of living allowed the blacks. When Alan Paton wrote of "the lovely land that man cannot enjoy," he was thinking of white man and black man and all shades in between.

It is a universal phenomenon of oppression that the oppressed see their circumstances more clearly than the oppressors. The white South African goes through a series of ideological contortions to explain what he takes to be the inevitabilities of his situation. But ideology is a luxury for the African, who has seen his last illusions about the good intentions of the whites methodically shattered. Since nothing but generosity would surprise him any longer, there is nothing left to explain. His exasperation can easily be mistaken for fatalism. But he is laconic simply because it was all said long ago and the saying of it did no good; also because he knows how dangerous speech can be. "This is a rubbish country," a black woman said to me with tears in her eyes by way of preface, exposition, and summing up.

Even the few Africans who are paraded by the Government as proponents of its policy of so-called "separate development" are careful not to get caught mouthing the ideological justification of the whites, at least when they are speaking to their own people. I once heard an explanation of "separate development" by the most eminent of its black spokesmen, Kaiser Matanzima, chief minister of the Transkei, the first of the "Bantu homelands," or states within the state, which the Government is establishing. His audience was a group of sophisticated Johannesburg Africans who were not about to accept the leadership of a tribal chief. Yet they couldn't help but be impressed by the deference Matanzima was able to extract from the white authorities; here was a man who had a good thing going. What he offered them was pure calculation. The only alternative to "separate development" was "the battlefield," he said. "In the Transkei we are afraid of that alternative. If you in the towns feel you can do so, you can do so and we will witness your doing it. And if the results will be in your favor, then they will be in our favor, for we all belong to the same race." With such friends, white South Africa obviously has no need of enemies.

I can think of only one occasion when I heard a good word from black men for the status quo in South Africa. The setting was a closed courtroom in Port Elizabeth where fifty-six rural Africans were being tried en masse for belonging to a terrorist organization called Poqo (meaning "only" or "pure"). The accused, who represented about one-fifth of the black men in a small Eastern Cape farming town called Steynsburg, sat almost immobile on the benches of what normally would have been the white and black public galleries, with large placards hung on their chests numbered from 1 to 56. For the judge's convenience they were seated in sequence. It was an overpowering sight. There were young boys and old men with white hair, schoolteachers wearing hornrimmed glasses and neckties, farm laborers in rags and tatters. I found it impossible to look away and as I stared I imagined the formal class photograph that should have been taken of this group—a grainy black-and-white image with the faces distinct and individual above the impersonal numerals. Of all the everyday scenes of the black man's life in South Africa, this one—the black man in the dock—was the one Ernest Cole had to forego.

The men from Steynsburg looked too undernourished to be effective terrorists; there was no

evidence, in fact, that they had ever managed to terrorize anyone. The prosecutor's gambit was to prove they had been dissatisfied with their lot. The accused, realizing that any confession of unhappiness might be submitted as evidence that they were likely Poqo members, strongly denied this. Here is the exchange Number 23 had with the prosecutor that morning:

"You have no objection to being ordered around by whites?"

"I have become so satisfied that my health keeps improving."

"Are you satisfied with your wages?"

"I have never complained—not on a single day."

"Do you want better wages?"

"No, your worship."

"Are you satisfied with your house?"

"It's a very beautiful house."

"Are you satisfied with the pass laws?"

"Yes, entirely."

The prosecutor, a scornful, sallow young man hidden behind a big mustache, found these answers completely unbelievable, as did every other white person in the room. Indeed, his questions would never have been asked had he been uncynical enough to believe the kind of answers they elicited.

Not only do Africans refuse to take seriously the murky set of rationalizations that make up the prevailing white ideology, they cannot believe that the whites themselves are at all in earnest about them. The blacks have no trouble unraveling the motives of the whites; they expect them to hold on to power and the riches of the land as long as they can. What they cannot understand— if, indeed, there is anything about the whites they cannot understand—is the very process of rationalization that leads the ruling minority on to new refinements of a system in which its power was long ago made as secure as it is ever likely to be. The result of these refinements is a kind of "overkill."

Why, for instance, can't a man who was born in Johannesburg and will probably die there be granted a secure right in law to remain where he is going to remain anyhow on sufferance? The white answer is that he might ask for the vote and there would be no valid reason for denying it. It would then have to be admitted that he was being denied the vote for an invalid reason, that expediency was all that influenced the value of black rights on the white exchange. How much cleaner it seems to avoid the dilemma by calling the man a transient instead of recognizing him as a resident.

Even if it is conceded that the black resident of Johannesburg is a transient, why does it have to be made well-nigh impossible for him to marry a black girl from nearby Vereeniging and live with her in Soweto? The Alice-in-Wonderland answer is that the white authorities have decided that the black population of Johannesburg has to be held down or it will begin to get the idea that it is permanent. The best way to hold it down is to inhibit the establishment of new families. This kind of logic cannot be pursued thoroughly or consistently. It would have to be really logical for that to be possible. But at least it can be pursued ruthlessly and remorselessly, and that the South African authorities are certainly doing. For instance, they are now razing the entire township of Alexandra, where about eighty thousand persons have been living in uncomfortable proximity to the white suburbs of northern Johannesburg. In its place they plan to construct huge hostels for the black men and women who work as domestic servants in the suburbs, all of whom will be officially classified as migrants. There will be no quarters for married couples. In effect, then, family life will be prohibited in Alexandra, all because the whites are unable to face up to the fact that the black majority in their midst is as permanent as the very land they think of as their own.

Theoretical abstractions are erected everywhere, opaque screens to hide the vast reality of black South Africa. When recognition of that reality is forced on them, most whites are quick to dismiss it with one of those pseudo-scientific simplicities that constitute their fund of knowledge about the African. I mentioned what was happening in Alexandra to a minister of the Dutch Reformed Church, Dominie Jacobus Vorster, an elder brother of Prime Minister Balthazar Vorster. How can a Christian people who like to boast about their mission work and con-

demn the secularism of the rest of the world do such a thing? "The Bantu doesn't believe in marriage," the Dominie replied with a wave of the hand.

Inevitably the new Alexandra will harvest an enormous crop of illegitimate children who will have no place in the white world around them or traditional African society. This should be a terrifying prospect for the whites. But it is just as inevitable that they will seize upon it for the chance to say, "You see, family life means nothing to the Bantu. Look at all those bastards! How can you talk about giving rights to a people like that?"

The problem, of course, is that black family life means nothing to the whites. If it ever started to matter to them, the whole system would become shaky. Almost every black maid in the white suburbs has children she farms out to relatives in some remote township or reserve; it is against the law for her to keep them on her white madam's premises. If she is lucky she gets to see them every other week or so. Maybe she has a husband. More likely she had one and lost him.

Once when I was writing an article about South Africa's fabulous gold-mining industry I asked the Chamber of Mines to arrange for me to meet a black man who had done well for himself by working in the mines. Out of the nearly four hundred thousand black men on the mines, they chose Joseph Wenene, a "boss boy" at a mine in Roodeport. He was a serious, soft-spoken man of forty-two, who might have passed for a back-country schoolmaster. He had first gone to work in the mines in 1941 for the sum of twenty-eight cents a day. (In other words, about three cents an hour underground; today a black man beginning in the mines makes about five cents an hour. Inflation!) Now he was earning $58 a month—about one-sixth of what a beginning white miner would earn—by working nine hours a day, six days a week, fifty-two weeks a year. On his pay he was supporting a wife and five children in the Transkei. They were not permitted to come to Roodeport and he had not been able to put aside enough money to go home. So it had been four long years since he had seen his family. "I am

happy on the mine," Joseph Wenene said gravely, "but my longing for my family is always there."

"You see," said a white official from the Chamber of Mines, who accompanied me to Roodeport, "he has nothing to complain about."

White unconsciousness distorts the African's life till the very end. One of the few businesses in South Africa in which black men can make a good living is the funeral business. Funerals in the townships are invariably held on Saturday afternoons and Sundays. One afternoon in a shebeen I naively asked whether that was due to some old tribal custom. "It's an old tribal custom of the whites," I was told. "If you say, 'Boss, I need a day off to go to a funeral,' he'd say, 'What's more important to you, your job or a funeral?' " People consider themselves lucky when their relatives die at the end of the week. It saves on costs.

An African has to be in his grave for his right to remain in the "white area" to be beyond challenge. In Johannesburg this existential license is dispensed on Market Street in Rooms 45 and 46 of the building of the Bantu Affairs Department (called BAD, for short), a dilapidated structure on the fringe of the financial district, in the shadow of the great mining houses. The long, almost stationary lines outside keep the building from being inconspicuous. All Africans must get on those lines when they reach the age of sixteen to apply for a reference book, the passport they are required to carry when they are in "white areas." The applicant must carry proof that he was born in the city and has resided there continuously, or he will be in danger of being "endorsed out," or "stamped out," by "influx control" officers.

Once he gets the reference book he is told to report to the Department of Non-European Affairs on Albert Street, where he must present proof of employment or register for a job. It is virtually illegal for an urban African to be unemployed. If he is, he can be "endorsed out" for being what the law calls "an idle Bantu." An African who loses his job must return to Albert Street and apply for "a permit to seek work." Without that he is again in limbo. Obviously a black man runs a grave risk if he is so independent as to quit a job, unless he has discovered a new

white employer who is prepared to fight his case through with the authorities. Usually it is better to stay with a job, no matter how bad the pay or working conditions. Thus the system reduces the black man to a unit of menial labor. South Africa has admirable labor legislation, but no African can ever earn the legal status or rights of "employee" as defined in those laws. The market on which his labor is traded is so anonymous that most employers record only the Christian names and reference-book numbers of their "boys," who aren't asked whether they have family names, just as they are never asked whether they have families, or where. The best thing that can be said for the system is that not all white employers fully exploit the tremendous advantage it gives them. But many do.

In their actual workings, the intricate rules are not universally applied. Very few new buildings would appear in Johannesburg, for instance, if the officials started checking the papers of the black workers on the construction sites. This doesn't happen because it is accepted that new buildings are necessary and desirable. Workers without the proper papers or no papers at all often have to live on the site itself. The official inspectors who don't inspect these sites are handsomely rewarded for their discretion by the construction companies. Most whites in South Africa would be astonished to hear what all Africans know: that the system is shot through with corruption. Some few Africans are sharp-witted and daring enough to make the system work for them, after a fashion, at least for a time.

But the best way to understand the system is to see how it disposes of its wastes. In Johannesburg this can be done by visiting the Bantu Affairs Court next to the railway yard, a low cement-block building with a corrugated iron roof that in no way resembles a judicial institution. No flag flies out front and there is no motto about justice over the entrance, not even a sign to say what kind of business is conducted inside. But the court is very much in the judicial business—on the penal side—specializing in a large volume and a fast turnover. On a normal morning a single magistrate can ring up eighty convictions before lunch.

The worst crime is not having a reference book; next comes having one that is not properly validated. Less serious but still serious enough to get a man chucked into jail for a week is having a reference book that shows he is not paid up on his taxes. The rhythm of business in the court is much like that of the other buildings in the neighborhood—the wholesale produce market, the abattoir, and the flour mill. Trucks back up to a big sliding steel door. The door is raised and a batch of prisoners is herded into open pens. When they have been processed through the court another truck comes up to the big steel door and hauls them away. Court procedure is more curt than it is in a summary court martial. If it were reduced any further there would be nothing left but the sentencing. The prosecutor merely states the charge. The magistrate then asks the accused whether he pleads guilty or not guilty and, occasionally, "Why were you in Johannesburg?"

"I was looking for my child," a man in grease-stained overalls replied one morning when I was there.

"Where is your child?"

"Lost."

"Fourteen days," said the magistrate.

Of the more than two million crimes reported every year in this country of only 17.5 million persons, nearly one-third are not crimes in the ordinary sense but crimes that only a black man can commit by being in the wrong place, with the wrong papers, at the wrong time. It is unlikely that there is any people in the world among whom a prison record is more commonplace than it is among Africans.

The impossible white ideal is to dispense with the services of black men altogether and return them all to their "homelands." But what is impossible for a whole people is easily accomplished in the case of individuals: Each African is replaceable and dispensable. In theory, black men are encouraged to rise above the menial level and distinguish themselves, so long as they do it in the reserves. But, of course, there is no scope for distinction in the reserves. In actual practice, the whole system is outraged by any evidence of talent or ambition or sensitivity beneath a black

skin. There is no black writer in South Africa today who has won any kind of public recognition. Invariably, recognition leads to exile and, just as invariably, the Government places a ban on publication of anything that has ever been written by the exiled writers. The last thing white South Africa is prepared to see black South Africa have is a voice.

No one can say that the Government has failed to be explicit about its aims. When the late Hendrik Verwoerd introduced the system of Bantu Education—which seeks to decree what a black child can learn, from whom, and where—he made clear that there would be no place for the African in the white community, except in specified forms of labor. His opportunities would be unlimited, however, in the black community Thus, it would be pointless to educate the black man to take a part in the white community, where he can never enter. In other words, the black man must be systematically disqualified for responsible citizenship in most areas of South Africa.

Dr. Verwoerd pointed out that the educated African feels frustrated because the country's laws exclude him from "the civilized community in South Africa, i.e., the Europeans." Bantu Education, he promised, would remove the frustration by removing the identification. If the black man refuses to consider a multiracial solution when he finally reaches the point of decision in South Africa, that will be proof that Bantu Education accomplished its aim.

For all South Africa's wealth, thirty per cent of the country's black children never reach school. Of those who do, only one in twenty-eight reaches secondary school. Four and a half per cent of the national income is spent on education, but only two per cent of what the Africans themselves contribute to the national economy is spent on the education of their children. At one time the best-educated black men on the African continent were South Africans. Bantu Education has exploded that boast.

Anything that sets a black man off from the mass of menial workers increases his vulnerability. In a pass raid, when the police start checking reference books, the well-dressed African attracts the most suspicion. If he is carrying a novel, or a briefcase, or a camera—as Ernest Cole was constantly discovering—he is examined with immense care and asked how he came to have such white accessories in his possession. The presumption is he stole them. An African in rags or a servant's uniform, by contrast, is usually above suspicion because his appearance fits the idea white police officers have of how an African should look. The first step toward security for a black man is the surrender of aspirations. Total anonymity and smiling compliance are the price extracted for a safe conduct. Nat Nakasa, a black writer who committed suicide in New York less than one year after going into exile, wrote before his departure from South Africa of the easier choice he could have made. "I could stop writing for newspapers," he said, "and find a comfortable job in the northern suburbs. I'm sure some 'madam' would find me intelligent and give me one of those incredible 'kitchen boy' suits—the ones with the pants that never fit anyone. I could bathe poodles and take fox terriers for walks in white suburbia. Nobody would know me."

But it is not only the creative misfits who have a painful time. Even without the humiliations of the pass laws or the great likelihood of fragmented families, there would remain the plain fact of economic degradation. Some Africans—prize-fighters, salesmen, doctors, and those small merchants who manage to keep on the good side of the authorities—may actually earn more money than some whites. But the general rule in any enterprise or organization is that the highest black man never rises higher than the lowest white. Even when this system of "job reservation" is stretched, as it often must be in a booming economy, a black man who moves into a skilled job will find either that it has been suddenly reclassified as "semi-skilled" with a corresponding cut in the pay, or that he will receive frankly discriminatory wages. Indeed, it is often true that white workers are offered bigger pay rises when blacks advance than the blacks themselves—to show them that black labor is anything but a threat.

White South Africans are fond of boasting that black men are better off in their country than anywhere else on the continent. They certainly

should be, but it is a dubious proposition, even when considered strictly from the economic angle. Though the black man in South Africa's cities earns, on average, only one-tenth of what the average white earns, he lives in the same price system. If he wants his children to drink milk, eat meat, and wear decent shoes, he must pay the same prices for these commodities as any white; perhaps more, because he may have to seek credit. Generally, instead, his children will drink tea, eat starches, and wear sneakers. The city of Johannesburg calculates that more than half of its seven hundred thousand Africans earn less than they need to provide themselves with basic necessities. Significantly, its calculation of the minimum income that most of these people don't have—only $77 a month for a family of five—budgets only six-tenths of one per cent for spending on recreation and amusements. Food, rent, and carfare take the rest.

However, many Africans don't have to worry about food, rent, or carfare. The miners, migrant workers in the hostels, and domestic servants all receive board and lodging as part of their pay. In most white households, the servants receive meat two or three times a week—"boysmeat," as the signs in the windows of the butcher shops describe the cheap cuts that white South Africans feed their help. Chicken is served once a year—on Christmas. Fruit and fresh vegetables are usually not provided and have to be bought out of wages that average about $6 a week. "Is it better to be a dog or an underdog?" a bitter African joke begins. The answer is a dog: "You get the scraps from master's table, but an underdog has to eat boysmeat."

White South Africans frequently illustrate the cordial state of race relations in their country by describing their relations with their own servants. But according to a publication of Johannesburg's Department of Non-European Affairs called "Your Bantu Servant and You," a large proportion of whites don't trouble themselves to call their servants by their own names. Sometimes they use a common name like John whether it belongs to the man or not. Sometimes the universal sobriquet of "Boy!" is deemed sufficient. The pamphlet deplores that practice. A servant,

it advises, should be called by his own name because "in his own mind he identifies himself with his name." Such insights show how much progress already has been made.

Because the whites have methodically used legislative and judicial means to strip non-whites of their rights, law-breaking has acquired meaning and value and even respectability in the view of many Africans. A young man arrested on a pass-law offense at the age of sixteen stands an excellent chance of becoming a housebreaker by the age of nineteen. The punishment for crimes like armed robbery are so severe that they act less as a deterrent than an incentive to violence. There is a percentage in murder if it reduces the chance of being caught. Certainly it is not mass paranoia that accounts for the burglar alarm signs on the gates of those fine homes in the white suburbs, the trained police dogs that slouch around inside, or the owner's habit of keeping a loaded revolver in the night table by his bed. The four hundred thousand whites of Johannesburg, it has been estimated, own more than one hundred thousand guns. Black men can't get gun permits, but it is obvious that they don't have to seek far to find weapons. In the year after the Sharpeville crisis, private white citizens in South Africa purchased more than ninety thousand guns. Since then, more than fifteen thousand have been reported stolen.

The advent of the police informer, however, has led to a drastic transformation in the style of African crime. In the old days the gangsters gave themselves and their gangs fancy storybook names and drove around in flashy American cars. Today a big reputation means the end of a promising criminal career. The security laws that enable the police to arrest suspected political offenders without evidence or a formal charge can be applied just as effectively against any would-be knights of the underworld. Beneath the cloak of anonymity, some Africans will tell you proudly, a number of brilliant criminals are making a handsome living breaking into white homes and businesses. During my stay in South Africa one such gang was rounded up along with a large cache of jewels and furs. The black gangsters, it turned out, were

all in the employ of a white "Mr. Big." There is no end to white overlordship.

There are other escapes from a life of poorly paid, subservient, unskilled labor besides crime. Selling out to the state, for instance. This too results from a faith in the efficiency of violence that is fostered by the whole system. Black men are increasingly prominent in the day-to-day operations of the *apartheid* machine, though their white superiors are never far off. Even the security police has its black officers, plainclothesmen who roam the townships in unmarked cars, stopping to make regular checks on the shebeens. These officers live in the townships, often in houses protected by high fencing. Prudently they make no effort to conceal the bulge of their shoulder holsters.

Both intimidation and financial enticement account for the large numbers of black police informers. It is relatively easy for the security police to convince a black man that it has the power to destroy him. It is also relatively cheap to offer him a higher standard of living than what is normally within his reach. The network of informers is now so widespread that most politically alert Africans can neither offer nor accept trust and candor in their relations with others. The few whites who seek friendship with Africans are also thrown on their guard. A black man can become suspect simply by living well without any obvious restrictions. More than any other factor, this cancerous doubt has killed off all underground African resistance.

I know something about this kind of doubt because I experienced it, I'm ashamed to say, in the early stages of my friendship with Ernest Cole. I had only been in South Africa a couple of months when Ernest showed up at my office, a slight, nervous young African with a pair of Nikons slung over his shoulder and a small sample of remarkable photographs. He spoke hurriedly, almost in a whisper, hardly pausing for any response. But he studied my responses carefully when they came. He told me a little about himself, waited to see how I took it, then told me a little more. He came back to see me often. He would call, ask if I was going to be in my office in thirty minutes and then take about ninety minutes to get there. His voice on the phone always seemed to have an undertone of urgency, but he rarely had anything urgent to say.

I didn't know what to make of him. My difficulty was that I hadn't yet recognized how thoroughly preoccupied, even obsessed, Ernest was with his one self-appointed task—the completion of the set of photographs that makes up this book. Our talks gave me some good ideas for stories and occasionally these were stories that could be illustrated by his photographs. But we didn't really have much business to discuss. When it was talked out, Ernest would tell me about his work and his endless troubles with the police. Not only was he constantly being stopped and forced to explain how he ever managed to come into possession of such expensive photographic equipment, but now he was also coming under pressure, he said, to act as an informer. He told me of his determination not to say yes and the danger of saying no. The best thing, he thought, was to stall. My experience of the world, such as it was, had not put me in a position to offer easy advice to someone with that dilemma.

But before long these conversations created an oversubtle doubt in my mind. Maybe, I reasoned, Ernest was telling me these things to dull any suspicions I may have had of him. Maybe, after all, he was an informer. Against this doubt I could always set the eloquent testimony of his work. That should have been enough, but the doubt lingered. Indeed, in vacant moments, I sometimes imagined that his determination to complete his work could lead him to compromise himself with the authorities in order to stay on their good side; that maybe he was trying to do as little damage as possible by informing on a foreign journalist who had nothing whatsoever to hide and who, in any case, was virtually immune to the pressures the authorities could place on South African citizens, white as well as black.

This may sound paranoid, but I was beginning at that time to pick up the first echoes of the Government's displeasure with my reporting. Soon the Afrikaans newspaper, *Die Vaderland,* was to carry an obviously inspired article headlined, "Foreign Journalist Abuses South African Hospitality." Someone told me—I have no way of

knowing whether there was any truth to the story —that the police had been making a check on me in the hope that I could be pinned with some improper act that could serve as grounds for my expulsion.

By this time also I had heard a number of stories about police tricks and impersonations. I had heard, for instance, of the ex-convicts who had been visiting the editorial office of a newspaper engaged in a sensitive, much-resented investigation of jail conditions. These unsolicited visitors would tell stories full of details even more lurid than those the newspaper had been able to uncover on its own. They would appear eager to dictate and sign a statement, but would always attach compromising conditions the newspaper couldn't accept, usually for a payment that might later be construed as a bribe.

I was to hear of many other such incidents. There was the case of the man who presented himself as a Yugoslav journalist, a most unlikely person to find with a South African visa. He later turned out to be a former member of the Pretoria police force. On one occasion, oddly enough, an effort was even made to impersonate me. A prominent woman in Johannesburg attending a political trial was approached during one of the recesses by a man who asked, in an accent that was trying hard to be American, if she could introduce him to the family of the accused. She asked who he was. "The New York Times correspondent," he replied.

"No, you're not," she said. "I know their correspondent."

"I'm their roving correspondent," he said, backing away in a fast fade out, presumably roving again.

The thing about suspecting that you are being followed or bugged or tricked is that you have almost no way of making sure. The suspicion itself is almost as effective a restraint as the real thing. One afternoon when I was preparing to leave on a trip to the Congo I discovered how much my own imagination had been working overtime. Ernest came by and casually asked what time my flight would be leaving and whether I would mind carrying out a letter he didn't want to trust to the mails in South Africa. I readily

agreed. But later in the day when he phoned to say he wouldn't have the letter ready in time to bring it to the office or even my home, but would bring it to the airport and give it to me there, my doubts took full command. Jan Smuts Airport in Johannesburg is anything but a private place. What if the letter were a plant and what if I were searched by the customs authorities? Feeling petty and mean, I made up my mind to take the letter from Ernest, but not under any circumstances carry it out of South Africa.

As it happened, he didn't get to the airport in time, so I never acted out my suspicion. Before long it disappeared entirely, leaving behind only an eerie sense of how close I had come to doing a serious injustice to a friend who all along had been placing enormous confidence in me.

It was the scope and strength of Ernest's obsession and what I learned of how it had come into being that finally commanded my trust. Ernest was from Pretoria. His late father had been a man of independent spirit who worked as a tailor. His mother worked as a washerwoman for whites. Ernest saw his first camera at the age of eight. It wasn't very special, but Ernest didn't know that. It fascinated him and he made up his mind that he would have one of his own. At fourteen, he took his first snapshots with an old 120-mm. Voigtländer borrowed from a neighbor.

Ernest quit school at the beginning of 1957, just before his seventeenth birthday. That was the year that Bantu Education was introduced in his grade. Until then he had been studying the standard South African syllabus. Now he could only expect a diploma that carried the word "Bantu," which seemed to him another way of stamping it "third-class." He decided instead to pursue photography seriously, and to finish his schooling by correspondence. His father was pleased by his act of defiance. His mother was frightened that he was cutting himself off from whatever small chance a black boy in South Africa has of finding decent employment.

But Ernest, who must always have been a hard thinker, had other ideas. His quitting school had put him in automatic and desperate need of a job. Wearing short pants and carrying school papers he didn't have to worry about police

17

checks; in long pants he needed a pass and a job. But his mother was right. He had little chance of finding decent employment. Ernest had a solution, but it meant running a big risk. If he could pose as a Colored he could step outside the pass laws and gain a wider choice of jobs.

South African law negatively defines a Colored as "a person who is not a white person or a native." The people who go by that name are a mixed breed with European, Oriental, and African antecedents, ranging in pigmentation from near-white to near-black. At one end of this spectrum many Coloreds pass as whites. At the other many Africans pass as Coloreds. Ernest was too dark to expect to have an easy time but he counted on two advantages. One was that his Pretoria upbringing had made him perfectly fluent in Afrikaans, the language most Coloreds speak. The other, as he put it to me once, was that "no white man in South Africa thinks a black man can outsmart him."

Probably Ernest would have resigned himself to carrying a pass if he had known in the beginning how many legal hurdles he would have to clear to become a Colored. He went first to the Colored counter at the Labor Bureau and applied for a job. He was eyed suspiciously there and told to bring a birth certificate that stated his race. Next he went to the registrar of births and asked for a copy of his birth certificate, although he knew full well that he was not listed there. To lend authenticity to his request he took with him a Colored friend who was willing to testify that Ernest Cole was an orphaned child of Colored parents. As Ernest had hoped, they were referred to the Late Registration of Births Office, located in the very seat of the South African Government, the grand and spacious Union Buildings in Pretoria, where the Prime Minister has his office. By this time Ernest knew that he was in deep, but turning back seemed just as risky as going on ahead. Each office led to another: The Late Registration of Births Office finally referred him to the Classification Board of the Bureau of Census and Statistics.

The men who work in that office are supposed to be expert at telling a white from a brown from a black—distinctions that are often hard to draw in South Africa, which is why it is necessary to require everyone to be classified and carry identity papers. Sometimes, it is said, these experts use what is called "the pencil test." If a man is black, according to their theory, his hair will be so wiry that it will be impossible to run a pencil through it. If he is merely brown, the pencil will pass.

Ernest was examined by a man who had too much confidence in his own powers of discernment to resort to that crude device. Instead he peppered Ernest with questions about his family and schooling, confident that he would be caught in a fatal inconsistency if he were lying. Some of the questions came three times, phrased differently on each try. But Ernest kept a perfect score. Finally the examiner threw what looked to be a change of pace but was really his best pitch. "How tall were you," he asked, "when you were eight?"

A Colored asked this question does what any Westerner would do—that is, stretches out his hand to the appropriate level, palm down. Africans indicate height with their palms up. The examiner assumed that this esoteric piece of information was known only to the Classification Board. But Ernest had been waiting for just that question. "I took all the time in the world to answer," he says when he tells the story. "I stood up so I could really do it properly." From that moment until he left South Africa, Ernest Cole was a Colored, palms down.

A few trusted friends knew Ernest's secret, but no one else, not even his parents. He continued to live as an African, but with considerably more mobility, a crucial advantage for him as a photographer. I once met a man who carried both an African reference book and a Colored identity card so he could be African or Colored as the mood took him. Ernest had the identity card and his dark skin, which was usually as good as a reference book when it came to moving about freely in the townships.

By this time Ernest was taking a correspondence course in photography from a school in New York and working as a darkroom assistant for a non-white magazine in Johannesburg. He had been seized by the idea of attempting to portray the truth about life in black South Africa, but

had not decided on the means. One day he came upon Henri Cartier-Bresson's book, "People of Moscow," a study of the daily life of the urban Russian, and realized that this was the form his story should take. It took him more than five years. Ernest realized from the beginning that he would have to leave the country before the book could be published. It seemed a big enough risk to have isolated pictures of his appearing in various foreign magazines and newspapers. Publication of a book would finish him in South Africa. In his last months he was unsure about whether he would be granted a passport. On his application form he stated that he wanted to go on a pilgrimage to Lourdes.

The night he arrived in London I took him out to dinner in a famous restaurant along with an African from Johannesburg who wore an easy cosmopolitan air after many years in exile. It was the first time Ernest had ever eaten in a good restaurant or been served by white men. I suppose I had some vague notion that this would signify a new beginning for him and fill him with a sense of freedom. But Ernest's head was nodding before the roast beef cart was wheeled to the table and when he was confronted with his plate he had all he could do to keep that tired head of his from drooping into the gravy. "London," he said with a big yawn, "reminds me of Fordsburg," one of the older, less seemly sections of Johannesburg. It was almost as if the script had been written by the South African Information Service: Ernest was homesick.

I recalled one of Nat Nakasa's musings about exile. "Life abroad," he wrote, "lacks the challenge that faces us in South Africa. After a lifetime of illegal living in the Republic's shebeens, the exiles are suddenly called upon to become respectable, law-abiding citizens. Not a law to break in sight."

For Ernest Cole, who never bothered to break a law unless he thought he saw a way to get some better pictures, the problem wasn't one of respectability but purpose. He had to recognize that no matter how he grew as a photographer, no story could ever mean as much to him as the story he left behind in South Africa. Exile meant the surrender of his creative obsession. Perhaps in ten or twenty or thirty years he would be able to go back to it. But now he was thrown on his own and forced to improvise. He was free and that was something, but he was also stranded.

South Africa may be a doomed and tragic land but it is a land in which a limited number of human values remains alive and palpable by virtue of the abuse they get. When I last saw Ernest he was in Manhattan. The same values that are abused in South Africa are abused in New York, of course, but less systematically. Our injustices lack the precision to which Ernest is accustomed. Perhaps that makes the values at stake less palpable. I'm not sure. But I know that too much moral clarity becomes a kind of drug and that sooner or later all injustice becomes tedious, especially to those who don't have to suffer it. Ernest Cole's photographs are important because they relieve the tedium and go beyond precepts. They are the raw facts of the matter, not just images of injustice. They should be difficult to evade.

New Delhi, 1967.

THE QUALITY OF REPRESSION

Today I think the split between black and white in South Africa is irreconcilable. The whites are certain that it is our heart's desire to be integrated into their society as social and economic equals, but they are wrong. The cruelty of *apartheid*—separateness—has infected us as well as them: We believe as fervently as they that there should be as little contact between the races as may be possible. For only by a separation more absolute than the most ardent racist could wish does there seem to be a chance of freedom from the suffering and oppression that living beside white men inflicts upon us.

It is a bitter fact that we have been slow to read the lesson of our history. Our anguish is in many ways intensified by the policies of the present Government. All my life I have endured them and, as I have never known anything else till now, they seem particularly atrocious to me. Yet our plight has been deepening for more than three hundred years, ever since the first venturesome whites invaded our land in search of trade, and stayed on to possess us.

At times in the past, our leaders were persuaded that there might be accommodations enabling black and white to abide peacefully in the same country. At times, as we learned the white man's ways and bent our backs to his tasks for the meager wage he paid, we were encouraged to believe that we might one day share in his future. How soon this happened, it was patiently explained, depended on us. As we overcame our deficiencies, lost our political and economic innocence, civilized our savage nature, and worshipped the white God, we would earn the white man's friendship and approval. Then would the best of us have a seat in his councils and the privilege of acting like white men.

Yet it has turned out that we studied the white man's language only to learn the terms of our servitude. Three hundred years of white supremacy in South Africa have placed us in bondage, stripped us of dignity, robbed us of self-esteem, and surrounded us with hate.

It is an extraordinary experience to live as though life were a punishment for being black.

No day passes without a reminder of your guilt, a rebuke to your condition, and the risk of trouble for transgressing laws devised exclusively for your repression. Some of these are merely petty and mean-spirited, others terrible in their severity and injustice. They deny the small comforts of a park bench and a drinking fountain, they make essential permits subject to the caprice of hard-eyed bureaucrats, and they countenance imprisonment without charges, drumhead justice, and political exile.

Legal indignities eventually become part of the reality of your existence—onerous, but unavoidable, and in a way tolerable, like a bad climate. What frightens and freezes are the sudden, direct attacks on yourself as a person. The white man's fear of blackness—and whatever it symbolizes for him—goads him unmercifully. His hatred erupts on slight provocation. One slip, one fancied slight, one ill-considered act or hasty word, and he is upon you, an enemy ablaze with rage and emboldened by his immunity. All blacks have seen white men and women thus. All have been tongue-lashed. Perhaps not quite all have been bullied, threatened, shoved, spat upon, slapped, or slugged.

There is no recourse. The protective institutions of society are not for you. Police, magistrates, courts—all the apparatus of the law reinforces the already absolute power of the white *baas* and his madam.

Your own people are as nothing. The strong father, the harboring mother, the blood brother—nothing. The loyalty of families, the allegiances of tribes, the many cultural denominators by which people may be claimed as allies in time of need—they are nothing. As social groups they have no status or influence. As individuals they may already have given in to lethargy and despair.

In such an atmosphere it is difficult to develop or hold onto a feeling of your own worth. Not only is your very being under relentless attack, but all your fellows are likewise under siege. You look vainly for heroes to emulate. The company of the besieged has a high casualty rate: Many already half-believe the white man's estimate of their worthlessness.

For want of anything else, anger becomes a motivation and a refuge. Superficially you must stay cool, however hard it is to do so. Retribution is swift for cheeky Kaffirs. But inside there is fire. You rise in the morning filled with sour thoughts of your poverty under the white economy. I remember days when I was so broke I could not afford the little gas I needed to go here or there to shoot pictures with the film I had nearly starved myself to buy. Whenever I could, I accepted invitations to the homes of white liberals for the food they offered—until it stuck in my throat at the thought of how casually they could regard it, while at our house we wondered whether there would be porridge on the morrow.

Wherever you go in South Africa oppression weighs upon you. There is never a day that your anger lacks for fuel. At its highest pitch you are shaken by its violence, and you feel you will go mad in the streets or commit murder.

But you do not. You make your own contribution to repression by repressing anger. Among friends you do not even talk of the outrages you bear. It simply feeds the flames. So you smolder but you do not explode.

Today implacable, unreasoning hate is a barrier neither white nor black can pass. Between them there is no glimmer of fellow feeling, no will to understand. What has developed in both races is a rigid and perverse psychology of opposites. Whatever the other says must be untrue; whatever the other likes must be bad; whatever the other fears and hates must have some value; whenever the other is decent, distrust him; whenever the other smiles in friendship, beware.

You may escape, but you carry your prison smell with you. Where parks are free and benches available, you do not want them. Good food does not impress you. Vacations are for fools. You do not try too hard or expect too much of yourself, for it is still a white man's world and you feel your difficulties are the result of being black. You boldly meet the white man's eye—and bite your tongue when it slips and calls him *baas*.

Your anger is unabated, for each day's newly discovered small liberties recall restrictions in the past. But as it flows—hot, strong, and unchecked—you know that in its dissipation is your first real freedom.

THE MINES

South Africa's wealth is rooted firmly in great mineral resources: diamonds, platinum, iron, copper, uranium, and, above all, gold. Gold was discovered a century ago and today the ore still pours from fifty-five operating mines. Most of these are located in the Witwatersrand of Transvaal, the ore-rich hills upon which Johannesburg, the "Golden City," has risen. So important is the Rand that South Africa has applied the name to its basic monetary unit. The mines produce about seventy per cent of the free world's supply of gold. In 1966, the output was nearly thirty-one million fine ounces worth nearly $1,100,000,000.

The work of mining the gold—and three tons of earth from shafts two miles deep must be sifted to yield one ounce—falls entirely to Africans. Twenty-four hours a day, six days a week, half a million Africans are at work in the earth. Of course, the mining companies also employ many whites, but all in supervisory capacities. Even those working underground, and designated as miners, never touch pick or shovel or drilling machines. The brute work is done by Africans, although they are never given the dignity of being called miner, only "boy"—or "boss boy" if they head up a work gang, the highest job to which they can aspire.

Labor for the mines works under contract and is recruited in the back-country tribal areas by mining company agents. Some men come from Lesotho and Botswana (formerly Basutoland and Bechuanaland), others from as far away as Zambia and Angola. It is one of the rigidities of South African administration that the mines are permitted to import labor in droves, but that an outlander who crosses the border looking for work is subject to arrest and deportation.

Recruits from all points are brought to the tremendous Witwatersrand Native Labor Association main depot in Johannesburg. Here they are processed and assigned to the mines where they will work for the duration of their contract. It was at the depot that I got my first look at this fundamental aspect of South Africa's economy in operation.

I was about twenty at the time, aspiring to be a photographer, but working meanwhile as a layout assistant for *Drum,* an English-language magazine published in Johannesburg for African readers. *Drum* was unusual in having a racially mixed staff and widely popular for its exposés of the injustices of *apartheid.* But the wealthy white South African who owned the magazine also owned mines. Thus, when the editor announced one day that the Chamber of Mines wanted to run an advertising supplement in *Drum,* we were asked to cooperate. The supplement was aimed at attracting new laborers to the mines and the editorial department was expected to develop a success story on an individual miner. It was not an idea any of us sympathized with, for we all knew how grisly the mines really were. But the publisher was determined, and soon a reporter and photographer were sent off to show how well a career in the mines paid off.

One day the photographer could not go and I was chosen to stand in for him. We were picked up by a Chamber of Mines official and driven to the WNLA depot. The official conversed easily with the white reporter and ignored me. To him I was just another "bloody Kaffir" with a menial job to do and he carried on as though I were not there. This is customary and you grow used to it. I would have been surprised if he had treated me any differently.

At the depot we passed through the main gate in the high brick wall surrounding it and entered a complex of office buildings, sheds, and hospital facilities scattered over an area.

The yard was swarming with African men. There were Zulus, Swazis, Xhosas, airsick Barotses flown in from Zambia in a mining-company plane, Shangaans from Mozambique, and Kwanyamas and Ovambos from South West Africa. All had signed on for a stint in the mines, although not many could read the contract in their hands. Read or not, each man was committed to an initial work period of nine months if he were from a protectorate, twelve months if from anywhere else. He would work nine or ten hours a day, six days a week, and his starting pay would be forty-two American cents a day. (That was 1961. Now it is up to forty-six cents a day.) The most he could look forward to, after many years in the mines in the highest grade he could attain, was $38, one sixth of the beginning pay

for novice white miners.

The African can be discharged, but he cannot quit. If he tries to escape he is branded a deserter and mine detectives from a special squad are sent to track him down.

"Actually, we prefer to hire these country chaps," the mine official said. "Otherwise we would have to compete with local industry in wages, and the urban African gets more money than we're willing to pay. The truth is that we are doing these men a favor by letting them work in the mines. That way they can supplement the income they get from their farms in their tribal lands at home."

It was a twisted picture, although with a measure of truth in it. The urban African may not be doing very well, but he makes more than the coolie wage of the mines and he will not take a mine job. The mine operators argue that they cannot afford to pay more because, while there is inflation in everything else, the price of gold ($35 the ounce) has not gone up in more than three decades. This cuts no ice with city Africans; the profit is there and the mine owners are neither ill-housed, ill-clothed, or ill-fed. They have assured themselves a never-ending supply of rural Africans and thus can get by without modernizing their equipment, upgrading their people, or paying decent wages.

So it is that labor comes to the WNLA depot, contract in hand, ready to dig the treasure underground. That first day I saw them standing in their patient lines, some queuing up to be fingerprinted, others stripped naked for mass medical examination. Some had been issued a tunic and pants, the cost of which would be deducted from their first wages, and an identification bracelet.

Once a man has run the course at the depot, and completed the administrative procedures, he is assigned to a mine in the Rand or to one of the Orange Free State gold fields, and transferred there by train.

I resolved to learn more about the mines, and in the years that followed I made my way to ten or more big mine compounds in the Rand. Sometimes I made friends with an African guard at the gate who would let me in. Sometimes I showed up so often the guards assumed I worked

there. Once in, I was rarely interfered with. To the white guards, as to the mine official, I was just another Kaffir and they paid no attention to me. As a result, I had considerable freedom to see what I wanted to see.

The living conditions of the men who work the mines of South Africa are miserable almost beyond imagining—worse even than in the worst slums of Johannesburg. The miners are quartered in long, brick-walled structures with corrugated iron roofs. They live twenty to a room that measures eighteen by twenty-five feet. Each man has a concrete cubicle, the slab floor of which is his bed. What little furniture the common room contains—a few rough wooden tables and benches—is made by the occupants. Threadbare tunics and trousers hang about; it is a jungle of clothes. The most privacy a man can get is to hang a blanket in front of his bunk.

Plumbing is not only ancient but inadequate. Shower rooms are crowded with men trying to bathe while others do their meager laundry.

Food? Ask a man what the food is like and he says, "Like pig's food." At mealtime the men line up to have their ration ladled out by a kitchen employee who uses a shovel to slop the porridge onto their plates. Each man must show a job ticket; only those who have worked may eat.

Breakfast is at 5 a.m. and consists of sour porridge and coffee. Lunch, after the first work shift ends between 1 and 3 p.m., is *nyula,* a stew of cabbage, carrots, and other vegetables, and sometimes meat, plus maize porridge. Supper is maize porridge and beans. The men crowd into their stuffy rooms to eat or squat outdoors. There is no dining hall, although there is a bar serving beer and hard liquor. Whenever possible the men go outside the compound to buy extra food—corn meal, for instance—which they cook themselves.

Sunday is the mine worker's day off, but boredom makes this almost the worst day of all. Separated from their families, with recreation facilities almost nonexistent, the men mostly sit outside their rooms, doing nothing. Some sleep. Others take a walk or sew new patches on their ragged clothing.

To relieve the tedium, a number of men participate in programs of tribal dances—the so-called

"mine dances"—which are a big tourist attraction for whites visiting Johannesburg. The dances are said to be entertainment for the blacks, but the audience in the stands is strictly segregated, and somehow the dancers always end up facing the whites and showing their backs to Africans. No admission is charged, but this is no more than fair considering that the performers do not get paid and that the audience is told, by signs on the walls, not even to toss a few coins into the arena as a tip.

Technically, the workers are free to visit the nearby townships on their day off, but few do. They often are simple, inexperienced fellows and impressed by the florid company lectures on the perils of the city, with its rough tsotsi gangs and diseased women.

Thus their blank and indistinguishable days, their circumscribed existence, their cramped and inward-turning lives. With women unavailable, homosexuality is widespread. There is even a word in minetalk for sleeping with another man: *matamyola*. The mine officials condone and encourage this and raw jokes about *matamyola* are frequent.

At the end of his contract, the worker can sign on again, this time (and each subsequent term) for six months, or he may go home again.

If he chooses to leave, he is sent back to the WNLA depot, where he receives in a lump sum the money the mine management has been withholding for him. It is never very much, but it is a rare man who has set aside anything from his cash in hand, and it gives him a chance to reach home with something in his pocket. If he quits at the end of his first contract, he is given a bonus certificate which entitles him to a two-cent a day raise should he decide within six months to sign on again. If he waits longer than six months, or loses his certificate, he starts over again at the beginning rate.

There are many temptations in his path, however. The white traders who run the stores at the depot, and the licensed hawkers and peddlers outside, try every wile to hustle the miners and part them from their cash as they wait for transportation to the trains that will take them home. It is easy to tell those who are homeward

bound. They are distinguished by new articles of clothing, or a cowboy hat, and the self-conscious grins of emancipated men. The system proceeds and they are no longer part of it. They watch the action going on around them, trying to get accustomed to freedom from tasks and orders, and basking in the jokes thrown their way. At this point the hawkers descend. They grab a man's arm aggressively, or swipe his hat, and shout, "C'mon, brother. C'mon," until they have wheedled him into buying their shoddy wares. The appeal is shrewdly calculated—it is the first and last time he will ever be called brother by a white man—and it often works. Some merchants even employ white girls to entice the miners into their stores by kissing them on the cheek. Many miners succumb to these blandishments and giddily spend their stake.

The majority of miners reenlists when its contracts are up. Poor as a mine living is, for these men it is even poorer at home. One will tell you, "I'll be going home when the drought ends." But it never does, and life in the mines goes on.

Finally, there are the men who never reach their contract's end. These are the unlucky victims of mine accidents or of phthisis, a deadly and so far incurable disease of the lungs, which is prevalent among South African miners. In either case, the man is returned to the WNLA depot for hospitalization, cancellation of his contract, and discharge. The mine company arranges for him to get compensation, sometimes in installments, which presumably protects the improvident African from spending all his money at one time or in one place. But it also means that outstanding balances need not be paid over on a man's death and that, even in incapacity, a man does not have freedom to go his own way.

The scale of payment is frugal. For losing two legs above the knee, and thus his livelihood, one fellow I saw received $1,036, which was being paid out at the rate of $8.40 a month and was supposed to last him the rest of his life.

However they leave—sick, injured, worn out, or hale and hearty with the savings of twenty years' work at $38 a month—they are never missed. For as they go out the gate, there always are new men coming in.

Pensive tribesmen, newly recruited to mine labor, await processing and assignment.

At assignment desk (left) clerk's rubber stamp dictates mine where man will work. Below: Waits are tedious; processing may take two days, time for which men are not paid. Opposite: Fingerprinting is necessary step in issuance of all-important pass legalizing workman's presence in white area for duration of his job.

During group medical examination (preceding pages), the nude men are herded through a string of doctors' offices. After processing, they wait at railroad station for transportation to mine. Identity tag on wrist shows shipment of labor to which man is assigned.

Left: Section of Rand Leases
mine compound, outside Johannesburg,
where African miners live
while on contract. No families or
women are allowed. This is a
typical compound, with buildings laid
out in a square and only one gate.
Barracks-like buildings are divided
into starkly simple rooms (below)
with bunk space for twenty men. There
are no closets or cupboards,
so clothes and boots hang all over.

34

Left: Kitchen helper dumps food on men's plates with shovel. Diet is nyula, *a vegetable mixture, and maize-meal porridge served twice a day. Below: Miner sleeps on concrete slab, must supply own bedding. Storage is improvised. Cardboard punched with holes and hung from the ceiling serves one man as holder for his spoons.*

Miners are idle on Sunday. Some, like man with penny whistle, pass time with musical instruments. Below, right: Man stares at snapshot of his wife on tribal reserve, whom he will not see for duration of his contract.

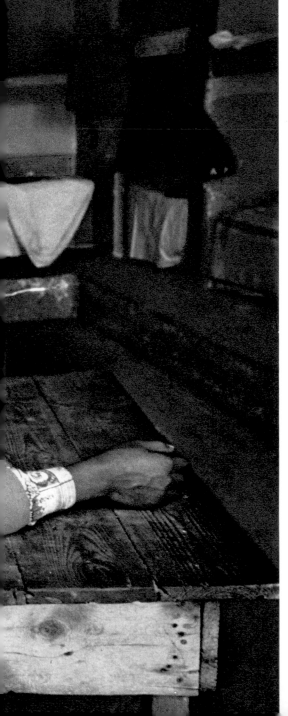

Left: Men going home. They leave with more than they brought with them: bicycles, foot lockers filled with junk clothing, blankets, other things bought at concession stores. As old group leaves, new one arrives (right), driven to mines by failing crops. Man with cane is signing on again despite wooden leg, result of mine accident. Below stands Johannesburg, Golden City, built by African labor and wealth of gold extracted from the earth.

Much of what is reported here and throughout this book will seem incredible to people living outside South Africa, beyond the confines of *apartheid*. When I say that people can be fired or arrested or abused or whipped or banished for trifles, I am not describing the exceptional case for the sake of being inflammatory. What I say is true—and most white South Africans would acknowledge it freely. They do not pretend these things are not happening. The essential cruelty of the situation is not that all blacks are virtuous and all whites villainous, but that the whites are conditioned not to see anything wrong in the injustices they impose on their black neighbors. The cold impersonality and righteousness of white supremacy are what make life in South Africa monstrous, and the ordinary standards of judging people's worth irrelevant.

The standard by which the police operate, for instance, is cruelly simple. To them every black man is a criminal suspect. In a technical sense, the police are not far off the mark to be so suspicious. The laws of *apartheid* are a far-reaching tangle of restrictions, reaching so deeply into everyday life that it is a rare African who does not violate some law. In fiscal 1964, some 2,200,000 crimes were reported in South Africa, which has a total population of only seventeen million people. One-third of these were not crimes in any moral sense, but crimes that only a black man could commit—by being in the wrong place, at the wrong time, with the wrong papers.

- If a black man sits on a park bench reserved for whites, he can be fined up to $840, or jailed for up to three years, or whipped (maximum: ten lashes), or any combination of the three.
- To qualify to have his wife and children live with him in an urban area, an African who was not born in that area must have lived there for fourteen years and have held one job for all of that time.
- The African worker may not strike. Maximum penalty: $1,400 and three years in prison.
- Any African may be summarily removed from the town in which he lives, should the Government decide he represents "surplus labor."

- The Government can cancel the employment of any African, for whatever reason, regardless of how long he has been so employed and even if his employer opposes the cancellation.
- Police are entitled, without warrant, to enter and search suspicious premises at any time of the day or night.
- A boy who continues to live with his parents after reaching his eighteenth birthday, unless he gets a special permit to do so, commits a crime.
- The Government may empower police constables to arrest and imprison a man without trial.
- A prisoner can be detained for up to 180 days without being charged.
- The sentences of political prisoners are, in effect, open-ended and can be prolonged indefinitely.
- Anyone openly critical of Government policies can be banished to a remote camp or be confined indefinitely to his home. Newspapers can be forbidden to quote such a person on any subject.
- Anyone who writes a message on the wall of a building advocating increased political rights for blacks is guilty of sabotage. Minimum sentence: five years.
- Africans may not possess firearms. Minimum penalty: five years. Maximum penalty: death.
- A policeman may at any time call upon any African who is sixteen or older to produce his reference book. If the African fails to produce it, or if his papers are not in order, he is committing a criminal offense and is liable to a fine or imprisonment.

The last is the nub of the infamous "pass laws," a complex mesh of rules and regulations that restrict the freedom of movement of Africans. Compared to some of the other oppressive statutes of *apartheid,* the pass laws on paper seem modest enough. But in practice they are the keynote on which enforcement of the entire *apartheid* system is based.

The African does not have the right to walk the city streets of his country. His presence in white urban areas is tolerated only as long as he is required to do his job. At all other times he is a trespasser, unless he has his "reference book"

with its identification card and a rubber-stamp permit to move about the white community. He calls this reference book his "passport to existence." Without it a black man is nothing. He cannot get a job, find housing, get married, or even pick up a parcel at the post office. He must have an employer's signature on his pass to prove he is working. Permission to look for a new job requires a separate permit. If a man wants to visit friends in another city, he needs a stamp before he can get on the train.

A man's pass contains his life history in brief detail. It tells his name, where he comes from, which tribe he belongs to, the name of his tribal chief, the place and date of his birth, and his father's birthplace. The pass also gives a history of a man's past employment (too many jobs, briefly held, can be a mark against him), tells whether he has paid his taxes and indicates his grade of employment—domestic servant, laborer, student, clerk, etc.

The Government can "pull" a man's pass at anytime for any reason, or for no reason at all. Simply by "stamping him out," it may expel him from the city, even if he was born there and has a home, job, and family there. Such a man is "removed" to the tribal district of his forebears, even though he himself has never lived in that district and has no friends there or hope of employment. By keeping him in constant dread of losing his permission to stay, the pass laws succeed in their avowed purpose of never letting the African forget that he "doesn't belong" in the urban areas. They reduce him to something less than a human being; he becomes merely a unit of labor, whose only justification for being in the urban areas is to minister to the needs of the white community. When he ceases to do that, he has to go.

The African must carry his passbook with him religiously, twenty-four hours a day. If he is caught without it, or if his papers are out of order (if he has no job, for instance, or has not paid his tax, or if his residence permit is made out for a city other than the one he is in), the result is almost always a fast trip to jail.

You can expect to be challenged for your pass practically every day. During a "blitz" as many as twenty-five hundred police sweep the streets checking passes, and you may be stopped a hundred times.

The pass laws help to breed insecurity early in an African's life. A schoolboy under sixteen doesn't need a pass, but as he grows taller and puts on long pants he is likely to be picked up. A common sight in the pass office is the headmaster arriving to vouch that his students satisfy the residence requirements and are legitimately enrolled.

One woman I knew had no legal existence in the eyes of the law. She had been born in one city and had gone to live temporarily in another. She was stamped out of the second city and then found that by leaving her home town she had lost her right to return there. It was as though a New Yorker had been ordered out of Philadelphia for staying too long, and was then refused permission to reenter New York. So she just drifted, and when she was challenged tried her best to explain.

Lack of a permit sometimes does break up a family. I knew of one young woman who came from the nearby city of Vereeniging to marry a Johannesburg man. She got permission to work and took a job there. Later she quit to be a housewife. Eventually she wanted to resume work and went to apply for new papers. "Aha," the authorities said, "you haven't worked in more than three months. Have you been having a baby? No? Then you have no excuse for not working and have lost your right to stay in Johannesburg." Married or not, she was stamped out of town.

To get his first pass, the young African applies to the Commissioner of Bantu Affairs. Except for a long line he normally encounters little difficulty here. To get the rubber-stamp permit he needs, however, he must go to the Office of Influx Control. Here he waits in another long, slow line; at the end of it decisions vitally affecting his future will be casually made. In order to stay in the area, he must have papers from the white official in charge of the township certifying that he has been a legal resident there since birth. These must be supported by a document from his school confirming his residence. And he must have his baptismal certificate and proof of employment. His mother must appear for interrogation, which often becomes abusive, for the petty functionaries

think that shouts and curses will rattle black women into blurting out any truth they may be hiding.

But if the mother stands her ground, and the son's papers are in order, his permit will be granted. If anything goes wrong, he will be stamped out.

Permits to hunt for a job also are issued by the Influx Control Office. The Government uses the permits to regulate the flow of incoming black labor. Such permits are usually valid for seven or fourteen days. If a man fails to find the job he wants in that time, he can apply to have the permit renewed. The authorities may renew it or they may arbitrarily assign the man to a job—any job that needs filling at that moment. Employers who are personally unpopular with their help or have "unpopular" jobs that they know they can't fill any other way, use the Influx Control Office as their employment agency. If a man refuses to take the job assigned, he is stamped out of town. If he accepts, even temporarily, he is "graded" to fit the job. An experienced clerk, for instance, may be classified "domestic servant" and his papers so stamped. Then he may well be stuck with that kind of employment all the rest of his life.

Unless he is employed, or has a job-hunting permit, the African's freedom is short-lived. In Croesus, the big industrial area in Johannesburg, men and women looking for jobs arrive early, even before the plants open. But the police are also on the scene early, checking passes. They arrest the unemployed for vagrancy even as they stand waiting for the hiring office to open.

Most pass arrests are made by policemen who are themselves black. These African cops are resented by urban Africans as much or more than the white ones. The police like to recruit Africans fresh from the rural areas, country boys. Naturally, such a man feels nervous and insecure in the city. But his uniform and the authority it gives him are his big chance to show he is somebody—not just a country lug. White superiors successfully brainwash black cops into believing it is a sin not to carry a reference book. "I have *my* pass," the black cop tells you righteously. "Why don't you have yours?" The inherent insult of the pass system does not occur to him.

I developed my own style of how to respond to the daily pass challenge, especially when it came from a white cop. I learned that you must grab quickly inside your coat for the pass and hand it to him without a word. Then he gives it back to you and lets you go. But if perhaps you are well-dressed and you know your pass is in order and you casually take it out and hand it to him with any trace of self-confidence—aha!—then he is liable to throw the book back in your face or slap it down into the dust. That is his way of trying to provoke you into saying something, anything, that will give him an excuse to pull you in and, if it comes to that, beat you up. He can charge you with "failing to produce on demand," which itself is an offense, even if your papers are in order.

Pass offenses are the one crime for which no official docket has to be made up. No witness is necessary and the arresting officer does not even have to appear in court. If arrested during a pass raid, the African must endure the humiliating experience of being handcuffed and marched through the city or township for all to see as the policeman goes about collecting new prisoners. The parade continues until the policeman runs out of handcuffs, or decides to quit for the day. Then he is taken to the neighborhood police station and held overnight. Next morning he is moved by van to the special Bantu Commissioner's Court—each city has one—which deals solely with pass offenses. Anyone arrested on a Friday must wait out the weekend in jail until the court reconvenes on Monday.

Each weekday morning vans from all over the city and surrounding townships converge on the court building. There they deposit prisoners of both sexes by the hundreds, as many as eight hundred in a single day following a particularly ambitious blitz. A crowd of Africans mills around the outside gate. They are friends and relatives of the prisoners, looking for a missing husband or father, waiting with cash to pay his fine or at least to slip him some food to take along to prison. If loved ones are not there in person to see a prisoner taken in for trial, they may never know what happened to him. So many prisoners are processed through that after sentencing they are almost impossible to trace. *continued on page 51*

Handcuffed blacks were arrested for being in white area illegally.

During a "swoop," police
are everywhere, checking passes.
Left: Young boy is stopped
for his pass as white plainclothesman
looks on. Checks go on in the
townships, too. Below: A student who
said he was going to fetch
his textbook is pulled in. To prove
he was still in school he
showed his fountain pen and ink-stained
fingers. But that was not
enough; in long pants he looked
older than sixteen.

Pass raid outside Johannesburg
station. Every African must show his pass
before being allowed to go about his
business. Top, right: Police check passes
for employer's signature, proof that
taxes are paid, and legality of presence
in white area. Sometimes (middle)
check broadens into search of a man's
person and belongings. Bottom:
White policeman oversees check of one man's
documents, while another, who said
he forgot his pass, stands by handcuffed.

Left: Every morning, police trucks from all over the city and surrounding townships converge on Bantu Commissioner's court building and dump their loads of pass offenders to await trial. Relatives of the arrested come to door of jail (below, left). Some bring money for fines, others bring food.

Right: Men who have finished their sentences depart under guard for their home towns. Below: People line up at Bantu Administration building to apply for passes. Line starts forming at 5:30 a.m., and latecomers may not get in. Without passes they are liable to arrest.

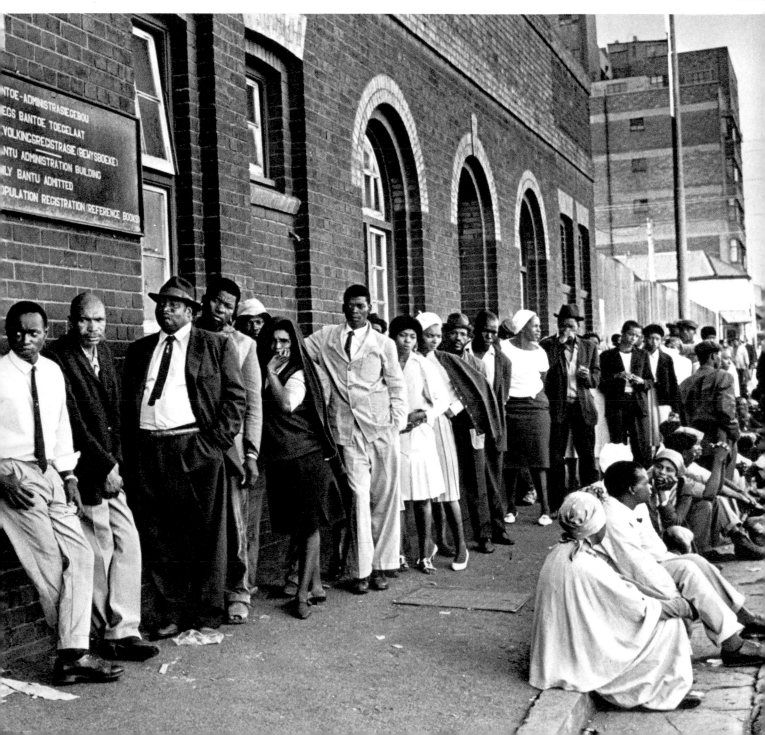

Even in court the African must wait. But once his turn comes, justice is swift. The prisoners are led into the courtroom in small groups and one at a time they are called forward. A trial may take only a few seconds, rarely more than a minute or two. This way the magistrate can handle nearly a hundred cases before lunch and still take an hour's break for tea. No defense lawyer is present and, except for compiling a batting average close to 1.000, the prosecution has little chance to shine. Usually an interpreter is present, regardless of whether the magistrate and the prisoner speak the same language. The charge is read and the magistrate asks, "Guilty or not guilty?" The interpreter rapidly repeats the charge in dialect and adds some advice of his own: "Answer 'Your honor, I'm guilty.'" Almost invariably the defendant answers as he is told and the magistrate pronounces sentence: so many months or so many dollars. If a man has the money, he pays his fine and goes home. If not, he must go to jail. A few plead not guilty and try to explain. But neither the interpreter nor the magistrate is much interested, and the man, still talking, is almost always packed off with the others. Usually the sentence is only for a fortnight or two. But if the charge includes vagrancy, the prisoner is in trouble. In the U. S., vagrancy is a minor crime, a misdemeanor chargeable against persons with "no visible means of support." In South Africa, it means a black who is unemployed, or does not have his employer's signature in his reference book, and can have serious consequences. When the magistrate sees that a man's pass lacks the employer's signature, he demands to know, "How do you live?" If the answer is not satisfactory, the defendant may be jailed for as much as two years, and on his release be escorted out of the area.

To avoid this, Africans who are in danger of being arrested often throw their passbooks away. Far better to be picked up for "losing" or "forgetting" your pass than for the unforgivable sin of unemployment.

On any day the prison population of South Africa totals seventy thousand men and women—almost four-fifths of them black. Per capita, this is almost four times as many prisoners as in the United States. Penalties are harsher, too. In 1965 124 prisoners were hanged—all but two of them non-white. By comparison, in the U. S. only one prisoner received capital punishment in 1966.

One fine old British custom survives in South Africa's penal system: the whip. In 1963, according to records meticulously kept, 83,206 lashes were meted out to 17,404 prisoners.

The bulk of the prison population is in for pass-law offenses and like as not they will serve their terms toiling in the fields of a Boer farmer, pulling up potatoes with their fingers. Boer farmers need cheap labor and it is a convenience that the Boer-dominated Government has a steady supply of prisoners available for rent at low cost. The Government turns over the prisoner's passbook to the farmer who has rented him, which in effect gives the farmer life-and-death control over the man. I choose those words carefully. Farmers have been known to beat their prisoners to death; if challenged they can always say the man tried to run away. In 1958, bad treatment of prisoners on farms was exposed in a public scandal, but it still goes on. I attended the funeral of one young man—Mokgoko was his name—who left his home in the township one day to go into the city. He never came back. It turned out he had forgotten his pass, was arrested and sentenced to serve his time on a Boer farm. While there he was beaten to death and quietly buried. A friend who had been pulled in with Mokgoko managed to run away and told his family what had happened. His family engaged lawyers who got the police to investigate. They found Mokgoko's body on the farmer's land, and—rotting—he came home at last.

Was anything done to the farmer? No. Killing an African is not a serious offense in South Africa.

But for an African to protest against the degrading pass laws can be a deadly offense. On March 21, 1960, a crowd of blacks gathered in Sharpeville, a town not far south of Johannesburg, to conduct a peaceful, unarmed protest against these despised laws. A scuffle broke out between the demonstrators and the police. By the time it quieted down, sixty-eight African men, women, and children had been shot and killed by the police in what is now known as the Sharpeville Massacre.

These boys were caught trespassing in a white area.

BLACK SPOTS

In South Africa today a "black spot" is an African township marked for obliteration because it occupies an area into which whites wish to expand. The township may have been in existence for fifty years and have a settled population of twenty-five or fifty or seventy-five thousand people. Nonetheless, if the whites so decree, it can literally be wiped off the map and its people relocated in Government-built housing projects in remote areas.

Action is not taken under the right of eminent domain, for this old and well-understood principle of common law permits a government to appropriate property only for "necessary public use" and requires that "reasonable compensation" be paid. In South Africa, relocation serves only the repressive minority policy of *apartheid* and compensation is much less than reasonable.

Authority for relocation lies in the so-called Group Areas Act of 1950, a complicated piece of legislation, many times amended, whose purpose is to assure that each of the country's racial groups shall live in isolation from the others; that non-white businesses shall not operate in white urban centers; and that the few property rights of Africans in urban areas shall be withdrawn.

Since the law went into effect, the Nationalist Government has carved the face of South Africa into a racial checkerboard of airtight black, white, Colored, and Indian squares. Hundreds of thousands of people have been uprooted in the process. Once an area is designated white, those disqualified by skin color from remaining there must move out. Africans who owned property have had to sell at disastrously low prices and move to districts where landowning was forbidden. Traders from the Near East and Asia, who were among the first to start businesses in many towns, had to close up shop within a certain time limit and start over in some location far from the commercial districts where the customers are. A non-white reluctant to move is moved by force. His house is razed, his goods hauled away in a truck, and the hauling expense charged to him.

Not surprisingly, the whites choose for themselves those checkerboard squares where they are already entrenched: the commercial centers and attractive, close-in suburbs. And any African township which seems to be standing in the path of progress they designate as a black spot to be taken over by expansion.

The Government pays for the property it takes, but the sums are paltry and often tardy in coming.

Sophiatown, a lively center of African life and home-ownership in Johannesburg, was bulldozed into a flat expanse of rubble. The new white township that went up in its place was called *Triomf*, Afrikaans for "triumph." Alexandra, another township on the outskirts of Johannesburg, is being converted into a vast hostel for unmarried domestic servants; there are no facilities for married couples. Eersterust township, near Pretoria, where Africans began buying freehold property at the turn of the century, was torn down and its

residents forcibly relocated. Lady Selborne, another old established township in the same area, also was being torn down in 1967, as this book was being written.

The Government describes relocation as "slum clearance" and likes to brag about its housing developments as the humanitarian solution to an "acute housing shortage." But the African knows he is only exchanging a "slum" that was home for the sterile prison of a Government ghetto.

Historically, the "acute" housing problem is one the white establishment has brought on itself by continually ignoring the basic needs of the black population. The whites have always told themselves that the Africans were transients in the cities and would one day return to their tribal homelands. Among other things, this has been a rationalization for paying low wages ("he can grow enough to live on back home") and failing to make provisions for housing ("he doesn't belong here, anyway").

Yet, as South Africa has grown, the whites have needed more and more black labor for commerce and industry and for domestic service. Blacks stream in from the outlands to the cities to join the labor force and become a permanent part of the urban population. Few—despite the white man's fantasy—ever go the other way.

From the start, years ago, a few of the blacks took the initiative, saved what money they could, and bought freehold property. The land area available to them was limited, but ownership was not yet forbidden. As more Africans became "industrialized"—became urban workers—the first black landholders shared their property with the latecomers. They set up shacks in their backyards and rented or gave them to people who couldn't find room elsewhere. Inevitably these neighborhoods soon trebled in population and, by Government standards, became overcrowded slums.

Even so, the old townships often contained a fair number of large and pleasant houses. Some were owned outright by successful Africans. Others were promotions by real-estate agents who made building loans to the occupants and took their title to the land as collateral. These occasionally were foreclosed when the family could not keep up the payments.

When the Government decided to move in, however, the good was destroyed with the bad, the large with the small, the expensive with the cheap. Furthermore, everyone ended up in a four-room house—regardless of the size of his family or his income—because that was the only kind the Government built.

Subsequently, those who were not satisfied with the Government's matchbox houses, and had the means to do something about it, built new ones in a small nearby area prescribed by the Government. Today these few nice houses on a few nice streets are the only relief from the prevailing monotony of the black townships. The Government never fails to show them off to tourists as proof that the African fares well in South Africa, although the guide forgets to mention that no black can own any land.

The white man, on the other hand, met his housing pressures by expanding outward and by paring away the black man's few rights of ownership and occupation. He not only made room for himself, but he effectively destroyed any permanent foothold the African may have thought he had in the urban area.

I had often heard the warning, "When a black township stands where a white suburb wants to stand, the black one must go." How true it was I learned one morning in 1960 when Government bulldozers came clanking down the road into the neighborhood where I lived. This was in Eersterust, a black freehold township ten miles east of Pretoria. Some would call it a slum and parts of it deserved the label. But I loved Eersterust. Our house was not fancy, but it was built of brick and had six rooms. (We also had recently erected a rental building on the back part of our lot with three two-room apartments. We had begun to get income from it, but were a long way from having paid for it.) I had lived most of my twenty-one years in that house, in that neighborhood. My father, a self-taught tailor, and my mother, a washerwoman, had raised their six children in the house. Most important, we owned the buildings and the land beneath them. In fact, the property had been in my mother's family for half a century, since 1910. This was no mean achievement for an African family. The property repre-

sented the labor and savings of several lifetimes. To us it was a proud heritage.

But under the Group Areas Act, our township was marked for demolition and its citizens for relocation. Actually, it had been declared a Colored area. An older Colored area closer to the city had been declared white and its residents were to be rehoused in Eersterust. The bile of *apartheid* flows downhill.

Once the bulldozers began their work, they were quick about it. Within minutes the black spot had been eradicated. Our neighborhood was rubble, our house a pile of bricks. For our heritage of half a century we were paid $840.

My family, along with all the belongings we could carry, moved to Mamelodi, a new black "location" which the Government had put up on the far eastern edge of Pretoria. (The term "location" is deliberate: Since the African is regarded as an abstraction, without status or meaning in society, his physical displacement is also defined vaguely, rather than in terms of an entity whose inhabitants have legal rights and real responsibilities.) There we were assigned to a new house. Like our old one, it was built of brick. In fact, all Government townships are built this way: row upon identical row, acre after symmetrical acre, all exactly alike. Mamelodi had streets, but at that time they had no names. Each house could be identified only by its number. They ran from one up to ten thousand and eventually, I suppose, on to infinity.

Sometimes communities are moved even before housing is ready for them. In Besterspruit, a farming village in Natal, some two thousand Africans were forced to move, despite the fact that the crops in their fields were nearly ready for reaping, and pleas by the town council that the Government township was not yet built. The Government ignored both problems. It simply erected two noisome tent cities, reminiscent of Boer War concentration camps, and put the people in them until their matchboxes should be ready. A black spot is a black spot.

We were renters, now. The privilege of owning land was forever lost to us. We had been poor before. We were poorer now. In Eersterust everything we could earn had gone to buy enough to eat. Now we had to worry about paying the rent, as well. Unlike the white tenant, who at worst may be evicted for failure to pay his rent, the African who falls behind is subject to criminal prosecution and imprisonment.

The Government had put a roof over our heads and, by its own reckoning, owed us nothing more. But any good farmer does better by his cattle than the Government did for the new residents of Mamelodi. The houses were incomplete and soon began to crumble. The four small rooms had no doors, no plaster, and dirt floors. There was no running water; it had to be fetched from a tank in the street. Toilets were outside and used the bucket system. Hired crews were supposed to pick up and replace the buckets every few days, but they were sloppily supervised and came only when they felt like it. In no time at all, the streets were a mess. The stench was suffocating.

In Eersterust we had eight food stores in our immediate neighborhood to choose among. In Mamelodi the nearest shopping center was a half mile away and offered a much poorer selection.

Worst of all, the destruction of Eersterust had smashed the relationships we had enjoyed with our neighbors. Friends of many years' standing went out of our lives, for in Mamelodi we were not permitted to settle down with neighbors of our own choosing unless they happened to be of the same tribal background. Since we were Pedi, we were assigned to one area; our Venda, Ndebele, and Zulu friends went elsewhere, and our Indian neighbors were sent to another township. At that, we were better off than the families that were split up. Unless a man had lived in Pretoria and worked for the same employer for a certain length of time, he did not qualify for a house in Mamelodi. Since he could not provide a home for his family, he was sent to a bachelors' hostel and his wife and children exiled to a tribal area.

The homemaking instinct is strong. In time we rebuilt our lives. But it was never the same, for with Government housing came Government supervision. Mamelodi was run by a white superintendent with the assistance of a corps of subofficials and municipal police to check on passes and enforce the laws. Whatever we did and wherever we went, white men's eyes were watching.

Child's home, in area declared a "black spot," has been destroyed.

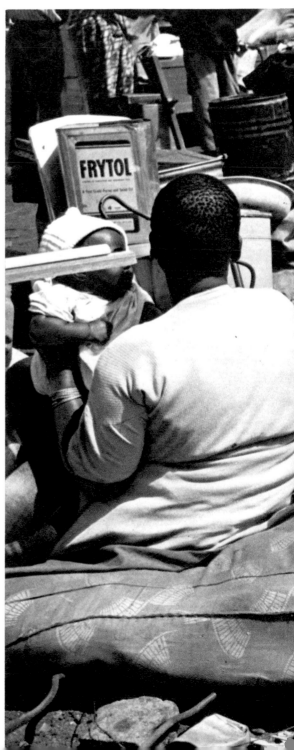

African township is bulldozed out of existence to make way for white expansion. Government trucks will move residents and their few possessions to matchbox houses in new locations, usually in remote areas, perhaps not even named on map. Even to live there, families must qualify. People at right did not, and thus have not only had their homes razed, but have nowhere to go.

*Left: Community
of two thousand people,
uprooted before new
township was ready for them,
was moved into tent
city, instead. Child
sleeps outside rather than
under stifling canvas.
Above: Typical location
has acres of
identical four-room houses
on nameless streets.
Many are hours by train
from city jobs.
Sign warns that permits are
needed to enter location.*

NIGHTMARE RIDES

Getting to or from Johannesburg by railroad is a nightmare if you are black. Trains are too few, too full, too slow. Some African commuters must leave home as early as 5 a.m. to be sure of reaching their city jobs by 7:30. Some are unable to catch a train back to their black township before 7 at night. These people may never see their homes in daylight, except on holidays. Twice each day, at the morning and evening rush hours, the segregated station platforms are a bizarre sight. At one end, a few white travelers stand about, surrounded by space. At the other, a dense mass of Africans is congregated, crowded and compressed.

No physical barrier separates the black and white zones. At some of the larger stations uniformed police may stand at the boundary and muscle back the crowd. But elsewhere what keeps the blacks from spilling into the white preserve is the unseen power of *apartheid*.

Within the black zone every square inch is occupied. There is no room for more. Yet latecomers arrive and somehow they are absorbed. People are immobilized by the pressure of other people; it is like being buried in people. Their shoulders, hips, bellies, and buttocks press against yours. You cannot shift your weight or raise an arm or turn around without displacing the several bodies that encompass you.

Finally a train pulls in and the doors open. If it is a white train, the few white passengers step aboard leisurely and choose a seat, for perhaps eight of the eleven cars will be exclusively for them. If it is to or from a black township, all cars will be for Africans, but always they are jam-packed and always there are far more people than even the most congested cars can hold. The wave of waiting humanity surges toward the doors. Elderly washerwomen balancing great loads on their heads, domestic servants returning from a family visit, mothers with babies riding their backs in cloth slings, office girls, workmen from factories and warehouses—all elbow and claw to get aboard. Agile youngsters clamber through the windows. The unlucky ones still on the platform dash from door to door, hoping to force a way in. It is not amusing; there is much at stake. For many of these people it may be the only train that will get them to work on time, or home again before nightfall.

Within seconds the cars are full—every seat, standing room, even the overhead space where passengers literally hang from the rafters. Dozens of others have crowded onto the couplings between the cars or cling to precarious hand- and footholds on the outside. "Washing" they call it. For when a train goes by at speed these passengers look like clothes hanging on a washline. It is no exaggeration to say that this wash hangs on for dear life. In one recent year, about one hundred and fifty Africans were killed riding the Johannesburg trains alone.

The white conductor blows his whistle. The train pulls out. A last few desperate fellows try to hurl themselves aboard, as though hoping they will stick. But they fall away. The cars are carry-

ing some five thousand people in space designed for two thousand.

Africans have become commuters more by law than by choice. The law requires non-whites to live far from the white residential and business areas where most of them work. The idea is to keep the black population out of the city environment, but not so distant as to reduce its effectiveness as a labor force.

The answer is commuting. Every early morning and late afternoon Africans by the hundreds of thousands pour onto the Government-owned railways for the ten- or twenty-mile trek between job and home. Trains have a virtual monopoly on commuter traffic. Very few Africans own automobiles and most are too far to make bicycling or walking to work practical. At one time, PUTCO, the nation's largest privately owned bus line, operated a commuter run to the black townships around Pretoria. Such service was sorely needed and was well used. But the railroad, which is in effect the Government, refused to allow the competition. So bus service for blacks was discontinued, except on feeder routes to the railway.

Africans are the best customers the railroads have, a financial fact well understood by their bookkeepers. The Minister of Transport has admitted in his annual budget message that, simply put, black passengers keep South Africa's railroads out of the red. Total revenue from non-whites far exceeds that from whites. And each year the relative importance of the African passenger increases. More and more of them are forcibly relocated in remote districts, while more and more whites desert the railroad for other means of travel, such as their own automobiles.

But the "best" patrons are hardly treated as such. Railroad authorities plead that they "just can't cope" with the rising volume of black travel. Yet the same authorities proudly maintain white service at a quick, comfortable, and dependable standard.

The all-black trains to and from the townships run with frustrating irregularity. I have been a commuter myself and I also have timed the trains during a railroad assignment from a Johannesburg newspaper. Rush-hour trains to the white suburbs are rarely more than three minutes apart.

Similar trains to black-belt destinations lag as much as half an hour apart. If the train arrives already full, there is nothing for it but to wait for the next one.

The morning rush lasts from 5:30 a.m. until 8. Stations may be up to three miles from a township, and passengers, who may have no bus service, or be unable to afford it if there is, start walking to the depot early.

At 4:30 in the afternoon the Johannesburg factories let out and from 4:45 to nearly 7 o'clock, the scene is repeated in reverse. Weekdays are bad enough, but Saturday afternoons are impossible. Between the families coming to the city to shop and the half-day workers hurrying to get home, it is chaos.

On Fridays there is an added difficulty. This is payday and the station platforms swarm with nimble pickpockets and purse-snatchers. They pretend to push aboard like eager commuters while lifting people's pay envelopes in the confusion.

The nightmare rides that the African endures not only sap his strength but strip him of individual dignity. Yet as a disenfranchised sub-citizen he has no recourse. He can't vote to throw out the Transport Minister and to get additional trains, extra cars, and reasonably dependable service—because he has no vote. As a customer he cannot choose to take his business elsewhere; the Government has vetoed competition. If he were organized into a consumers' union he might boycott the railroads by refusing to ride them and thus scramble the business machinery of Johannesburg, which however much it degrades him, depends on him. But organizing boycotts is against the law. So he goes on numbly riding the train.

The railways probably will enlarge their facilities just enough to provide a bare minimum of service for the growing numbers of African riders. For it is important, after all, to get the "bloody Kaffirs" in to work. It is good business, too. Unlike so many lands, where public transportation operates at a loss and must be heavily subsidized, South Africa's black-supported railroads cost the taxpayer nothing. Instead, they turn a profit of $10,000,000 a year for the white Government.

Following pages: Africans throng Johannesburg station platform during late afternoon rush hour.

Left: With no room inside train, some ride between cars. Which black train to take is matter of guesswork. They have no destination signs and no announcement of arrivals is made. Head car may be numbered to show its route, but number is often wrong. In confusion, passengers sometimes jump across track (right), and some are killed by express trains. Below: Whistle has sounded, train is moving, but people are still trying to get on.

*Preceding pages: Train accelerates with its load of
clinging passengers. They ride like this through rain and cold,
some for the entire journey. Inside, hands cling to a
suitcase, a woman carries a baby on her back. All stand packed together
on the floors and seats. At end of ride comes a big squeeze
(bottom) as passengers must show their tickets before passing through
narrow exit gates. As they wait, more trains pull
in and unload. For many the delay lasts twenty-five minutes.*

THE CHEAP SERVANT

White homes are the crucible of racism in South Africa. Here the races meet, face to face, as master and servant. But unfortunately they do not mix. Nowhere is there more animosity than in the everyday relationships between household domestics and their employers. The Africans, for their part, are bitter over what they consider to be degrading treatment and poor pay. The whites are baffled when servants seem lazy, resentful, and ungrateful. White women, particularly, spend hours conferring among themselves on the problem, apparently beyond their powers of comprehension, of how to "handle" their servants. The employees of such ladies merely shrug and whisper among themselves. "When madam returns from her tea date," they say, "you can be sure of two things: She will be in a terrible temper and she will have a brand new recipe for handling her servants."

Needless to say, all servants under discussion here are black and all masters white. I have never seen or heard of a white servant in South Africa. Black help is abundantly easy to come by. In Johannesburg alone, there are seventy thousand black servants. Because they come so cheap, hardly a white family in all the land is so poor that it cannot afford at least one or two African servants. Even a Boer of the poorest white class, a railway line worker, for instance, will have a servant. On the job he may be only a laborer, but at home he's somebody's boss.

The middle class of South Africa is the most fortunate, compared to their economic peers in other nations. Families who would be lucky to afford part-time help—a cleaning woman once a week, perhaps—if they lived in New York or London, have staffs of five or six full-time servants in South Africa. There is an African for every job—cook-girl or cook-boy, washing girl and nannie, chauffeur, floor-boy, and garden-boy. Among them they run the homes of South Africa. They command bustling kitchens, manicure the lawns and gardens, nurse the white infants, polish the car, scrub the floor, and walk the master's poodle. Their labor frees the white housemistress to devote her day to enjoying the social life of her pleasant suburb, entertaining and being entertained. When she returns, her house will have been cleaned, her dinner cooked, her children scrubbed, hugged, and tucked in bed. One result of this abundance of service is that many a young white South African girl grows up and marries without ever learning how to wash a glass or to make an ordinary cup of tea.

The injustice in the situation is not that the Africans are servants, but that few, if any, of them are paid decently, fed decently, or treated decently by any standard of behavior that the white would apply to themselves.

Pay, pay, pay. That is the basic issue. There is hardly an employer who does not take advantage of his help. Typical pay for a live-in servant is $15 to $20 a month, plus bed and meals. A few earn more, many earn less. The employer's attitude is, "I feed you, I house you. You have no other responsibilities, so what more do you need?"

The answer is that almost every servant does have other responsibilities—sometimes a whole house full of them. Almost every servant works to support people other than herself. Manserv-

ants often have a family at home in the rural areas. Maids and cooks may have dependent children, either at home or farmed out to relatives. The typical employer pretends such dependents do not exist. It is literally a case of "out of sight, out of mind."

It is a wry joke among Africans that, for all the practice they get and the time they devote to talking about it, white masters and madams still don't know how to deal with their black help. The trouble usually is that the employer insists on treating the African as a subhuman being, devoid of feelings.

In getting my pictures of the way servants live I traveled through all the fine suburbs of northern Johannesburg—Killarney, Dunkeld, Illovo, Melrose, Melrose East, and Houghton—moving carefully, you may be sure, for whites are immediately suspicious of blacks they have not seen before, or whose errands bring them into the white preserves. Sometimes I had to beat a hasty retreat when some young madam shouted at me to get out, but by and large I was able to enter a great many households and interview a number of servants. Without exception, they were seething with anger, scorn, and resentment. I was quite taken aback. I had resisted going to these suburbs because I was sure that the servants of the rich were having a somewhat better time of it and would not be typical of servants as a whole. But such was not the case, and many felt so bitter that they had no fear of being quoted or overheard.

What is your madam like, I asked one experienced cook. "Rude, raw, and impossible from the core," she said. "And hard to please. Whites think that with their money they can buy everything, even your feelings. When they employ you, they tell you your duties will be this or that, but in the long run they make you into a shifting spanner [an adjustable wrench, meaning a maid of all work], bound to do every kind of job."

Actually, it was less the fact that some unexpected duty might be required of her than that madam invariably issued her orders with a peremptory, demeaning "You must..." or "You have to...." For what grinds the soul is that in South Africa madam is right. There is no escape from the indignity of compulsion. Servants may quit an onerous job, but there is no prospect of finding anything but another one, with the same long hours, the same low pay, and the same cranky, coercive madam.

Exasperation with the whites' seeming inability to understand their servants' position is expressed in a comment that is common currency among domestic workers: "If you don't complain, they think you're happy. If you do complain, they think you're ungrateful."

In the past two years, a manual, "Your Bantu Servant and You," has been published to advise employers how to live elbow to elbow with their servants and at the same time remain aloof. The book suggests that if employers would only "address their domestic servants by name, speak to them in a language they understand and try to remember that they are human, then racial tensions might be substantially reduced." Elementary? Not in South Africa.

The manual goes on to urge women employers to use decorum in their relationship with male employees. "Always behave toward them with the same dignity and modesty with which you would behave toward a [white] male of your own age," the manual says. "Above all, never appear before him in any state of undress."

On the subject of the "feeding habits" of servants, the employer is urged to add protein foods such as meat and milk to the starchy diets most servants get, and to remember that "most Bantu are used to taking their time about their meals."

As for working hours, the book continues: "It must be remembered that domestic servants are human, with recreational, social and other interests." Therefore, it is recommended that servants not be expected to work more than sixty-five hours a week. This can be accomplished by never working them more than ten hours a day and by giving them every Thursday afternoon off, plus every other Sunday afternoon. The manual points out that it is necessary to pay "good" wages to keep good servants. The "good" wage it recommends for a live-in servant is $22 a month. For a sixty-five-hour week that's about nine cents an hour.

The recommendations—and recommendations

is all that they are—would appear to set something less than a bare minimum standard for the relationship between any employer and his employee, but in practice they represent a top level of treatment that is achieved by only the most enlightened of South African employers.

In most homes the servants are treated ambivalently. During the work day they may be shouted and screamed at, but they are also accepted in the most intimate and responsible family situations. They cook and serve food and care for infant children, but once the work is done they are shunted off, almost quarantined.

Housing for servants can only be described as ludicrous and deplorable. It is against the law for a servant to sleep under the same roof with his or her employer, no matter how big the house. In luxury apartment buildings the servants' quarters are usually built atop the flat roof—a double row of connecting, cell-like rooms humorously referred to as "locations in the sky."

Servants in private homes live "out back," in little rooms separated from the main house. Sometimes these rooms are just a tangle of tumbledown corrugated huts and lean-to's. Only the newest and nicest homes, built with *apartheid* in mind, provide cold-water showers and decent toilets. In most homes the servant must wash herself in the same bucket she uses for washing the floor. Her tiny room is almost sure to be sparsely furnished, with a mattress of straw, newspaper for a carpet, and fruit crates for table and chair. The window will be uncurtained, and her few belongings hang from pegs in the walls, rather than in a closet.

The servant's work day is long, stretching from early morning at least through the dinner hour. If there should be an evening party—and with servants to do the work, such parties are plentiful—the cleanup job may not be finished until 3 a.m. But there is no extra money for overtime work. "We must be punctual reporting for duty," the servant says. "But there is no punctuality about when we may knock off."

If a servant lives in, her only time off is Thursday afternoon and alternate Sundays. Even on these days she may use up half her precious time riding the bus to and from her family home in the black township. The servant who lives at home and commutes must leave her own children shortly after dawn and does not see them again until evening. Why does she do it? Not to buy luxuries, I assure you. Even if she has a husband who works, she needs the extra income just to keep her family a step ahead of starvation.

Most employers go beyond separate housing and impose what I call "kitchen *apartheid*." They insist that their servants eat separate food from separate utensils. Everything must be segregated: enamel plates, spoons, drinking mugs, even the "black pot" in which the dinner is prepared. An African cook can prepare the white family's food, lay the table, taste each dish beforehand to see if it is ready, then serve it. But then she is supposed to disassociate herself from the "master's food" and the "master's plate," as though she had never had anything to do with them.

Employers must feed their servants and of course they try to get away as cheaply as possible. The standard fare, repeated day after monotonous day, is tea, bread, and jam for breakfast, and porridge and boysmeat for lunch and dinner. Boysmeat is the name given to the cheapest, least edible meat the butcher can find, cuts that no white person would dream of buying for himself. Boysmeat may be the neck of a cow, a pig's nose, the hoof of a goat, or some other equally unappetizing part. The butcher is free to use his discretion. When the lady of the house phones in her weekly meat order she simply says "send so many pounds of steak, so many pounds of roast beef and, oh, yes, throw in a few pounds of boysmeat." (The "boy," of course, is the male African the meat is intended for. In the eyes of the whites, no African ever becomes a man. Until he reaches his teens he is a pickaninny; thereafter, until he dies of old age, he is merely "boy.") Even boysmeat is served in portions too small to fill the stomach and almost never is it supplemented by such white staples as salad, dessert, or a snack between meals. Or even butter.

Because the African eats so poorly he has developed a negative, almost perverse attitude toward food. One African term for food is *ditshila tsha meno:* "that which dirties the teeth." Food is not considered something that one savors or makes a fuss over; it is the last thing in the world the

African wants to argue about. Rather than complain about food, in fact, most Africans just accept the boysmeat—even though both the name and the substance are distasteful to them. As a result, many a white householder, convinced that he is an expert on the feeding habits of "his natives," is sure that all Africans prefer boysmeat, just as all rabbits like carrots. It is a nice, cheap theory to cling to. How surprised such an "expert" would be if he knew that in the privacy of his kitchen, "his" natives exchange their food for the table scraps and bits of steak and roast intended for the family pets. Boysmeat is swapped for dogmeat.

The lady of the house may not know her servant's last name, or where she lives, or care when she is ill or has problems at home. But the lady does know how she wants her "girls" to look: as unassuming as possible. Standard garb is a modest uniform with hair tucked under a starched cap, for servants are not allowed to be bareheaded in master's house. On her half-day off, of course, a young maid may be as style-conscious as her tiny budget will allow. She may go off to town with her hair combed down, her nails polished, and wearing a well-cut dress. But many a girl servant learns the hard way that madam does not appreciate competition. "I don't want two madams in my house," the lady employer announces, and the girl who is "cheeky" enough to dress up is fired.

The servant's job is a lonely one. She is cut off from her family. No recreation facilities are open to her—not even a neighborhood movie or a public park. At day's end she can only go back to her room, alone. White families don't like Africans hanging about who are not part of their household. So the servant, unless she gets special permission, may entertain her friends only "on the other side of the wall"—on the sidewalk outside the master's property. Male visitors are especially unwelcome. A woman servant's every male caller, whether he be her son, her father, or even her bonafide husband, all are lumped together in the employer's eye as "boyfriends." It is illegal for a man and his wife to sleep together in servants' quarters unless they both are employed there.

For all that, there is little supervision or protection offered the young unmarried girl who goes to work as a house servant. Too often she is left alone at night in her barren room—lonesome, bored, cut off from the security of the main house. Perhaps she does not even have a lock on her door. Such a girl, willingly or unwillingly, will have male visitors. When eventually she has to report to her employer that she is expecting a baby, the employer's righteous response is predictable: "What else can you expect from these Kaffirs? They breed like rabbits."

In the long run, the employer pays a price for the shoddy treatment and low pay he dispenses. Little or no sense of loyalty develops between servant and master. The servant has no motivation or encouragement to work hard. There is almost no chance for advancement, so servants are constantly quitting or getting themselves fired. I have talked to dozens of servants, all of them still very young, who had already been employed by as many as ten families. Two months here, three months there—a servant can always get a new job, usually without even leaving the neighborhood. But the low pay and the antagonisms remain about the same from place to place. Salaries are due on the first of the month, but employers, hoping to prevent the servant from leaving, often stall the payment until almost the middle of the month. That way, if a servant walks out, he forfeits wages he has already earned. A nice trick, but even that barely slows the turnover.

One of the ironies of the system is the role of the black nanny. Though she is separated by her job from her own loved ones, she at least has the young children of her employer to care for and love. The visible affection that flows both ways between a nanny and the white children in her care can be a wonderful sight to see.

But even that relationship is doomed. Home, after all, is the incubator of racism. Children watch how their parents treat the black "boys" and "girls" and soon the youngsters realize that they can get away with the same conduct. Servants obsequiously call the children *klein baas* (small boss) and *nonnie* (small madam). The kids soon get to like this. The lessons they learn at home are carried into the streets, into office and factory and Government post. Thus the awful heritage of racism is perpetuated.

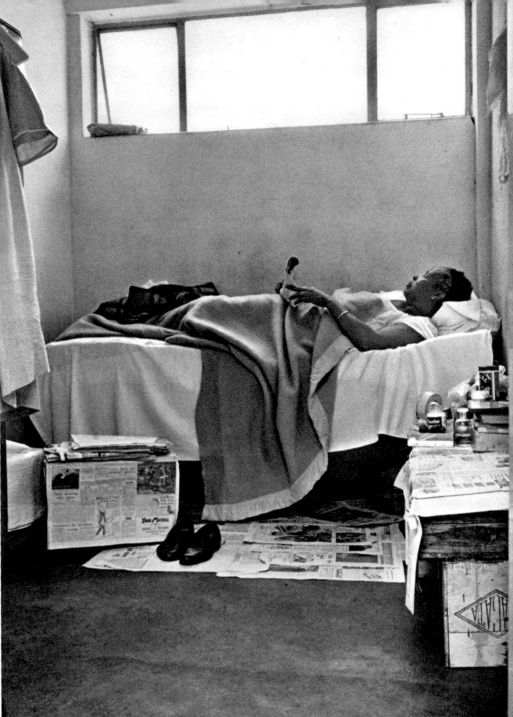

*Above, left: Servants' quarters
atop a luxury apartment house in
northern Johannesburg. It is
against the law for black
servants to live under the same
roof as their employers. In
private home, servant would have
separate little room in
backyard. Left: She lives on edge of
opulence, while her own world
is bare. Newspapers are her carpet, fruit
crates her chairs and table.*

Dogs are well tended by black servant,
and well fed. Above: Servants are given boysmeat,
cheapest cuts available. Everything connected
with eating is segregated: There are spoons, enamel
plates and mugs, even cooking pots specified
for use by servants only. Right: Servants are not
forbidden to love. Woman holding child said,
"I love this child, though she'll grow up to treat me
just like her mother does. Now she is innocent."
Far right: Entertaining friends is done outside
garden walls, since employers do not
want strange "boys" and "girls" on their premises.

*Living in her
"kaya" out back, servant
must be on call
six days out of seven and
seven nights out of
seven. She lives a lonely
life apart from
her family. In white
suburbs there
are no recreation
centers open
to black servants.*

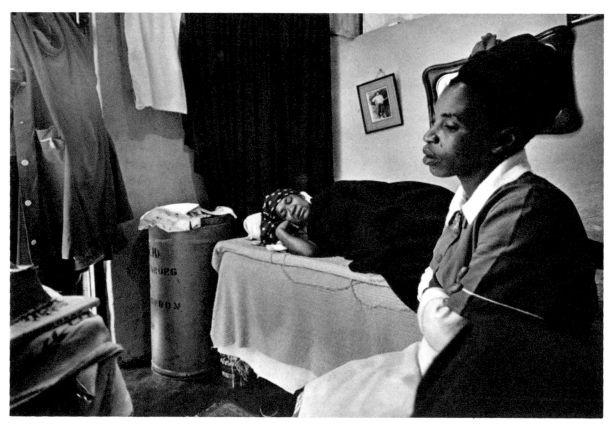

78

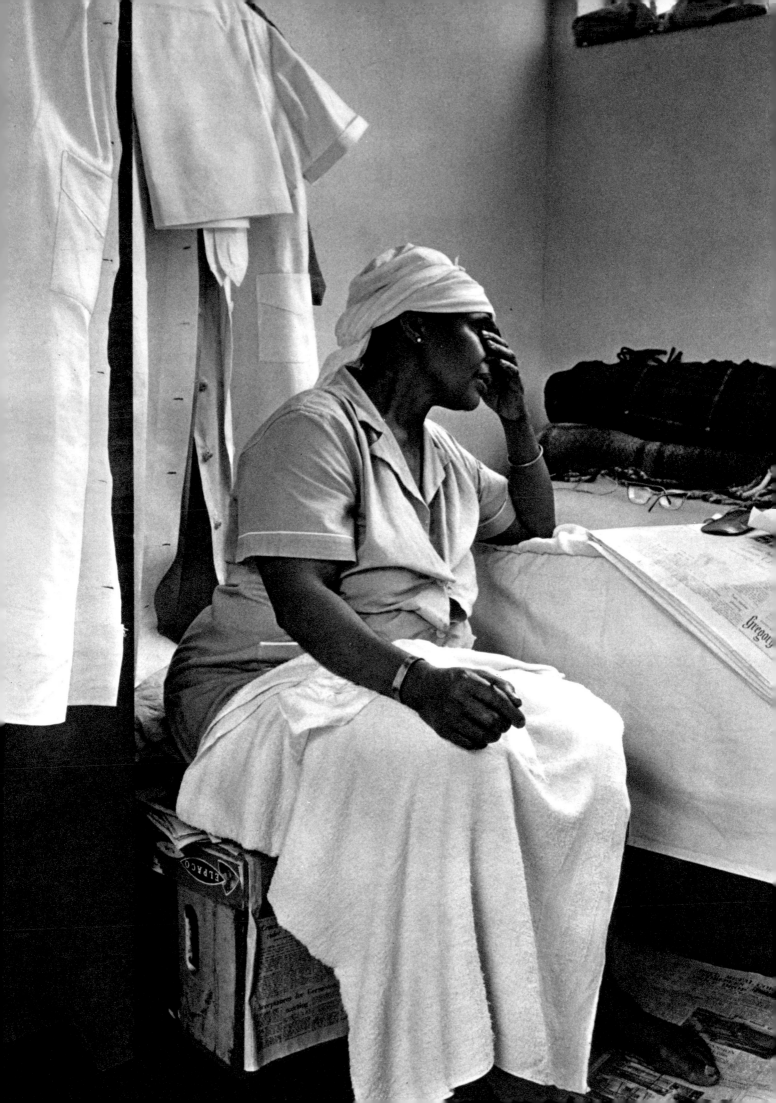

Left: On duty, servant
dresses in unpretentious cap and
apron. She must never
go bareheaded during work hours.
On off hours, however,
she may dress as fashionably as she
can afford. Girl in striped suit
lost two jobs because she was too chic.
Right: After working all
week in modern kitchen, servant
returns to her own, with
no hope of making it any better.

FOR WHITES ONLY

The infectious spread of *apartheid* into the smallest detail of daily living has made South Africa a land of signs. They are everywhere, written in English or Afrikaans or in a local native dialect as the situation may require. But always their purpose is the same: to spell out the almost total separation of facilities on the basis of race. Until recently the signs used the euphemism "Europeans Only" or "Non-Europeans Only." Now, as the Government seeks to emphasize South Africa's own heritage, independently of its historic European ties, the wording of the signs is changing to "White Only."

The meaning, however, remains the same. A stranger, freshly arrived in South Africa, might find the forest of *apartheid* signs helpful, even indispensable, in avoiding public embarrassment or possibly a tangle with the law. But to the African the signs are nothing but oppressive. They are always there, wherever he turns, to remind him that he is inferior. They shout at him that he is unfit to mingle, unworthy to enter through a certain door or to do business at a certain counter. And always the separate facilities for the blacks are poor. The lines are long. The buses and trains are jampacked because they run so infrequently.

The signs demonstrate into what homely corners of activity *apartheid* has reached. They point to racially segregated public toilets, to drinking fountains, phone booths, and station waiting rooms (where only one of anything has been provided, it is, of course, White Only). Post offices are marked with separate entrances which lead to segregated windows for selling postage stamps. Parks are often reserved for whites only. Those the blacks may visit have white-only benches. The African who wishes to rest must sit on the curb. In Pretoria there is even a separate railroad station for blacks.

Everywhere in South Africa it is unlawful for black and white to drink a cup of tea together unless they have obtained a special permit. At the blood bank, black and white plasma is kept carefully separated, although in an emergency the doctor would not hesitate to use whatever blood is available because, chemically, there is no difference in the blood of whites and blacks. (He'd never tell the patient, of course.)

The ocean beaches are clearly marked for color. A recent session of the Nationalist-dominated Parliament delved in all seriousness into the question of whether *apartheid* should extend to the high-tide or the low-tide mark. Either way, the M.P.s concluded that the Africans could wade across from black beaches into white water, thus "spoiling" it for white swimmers. The solution arrived at by the lawmakers was to use the precedent of international convention: *Apartheid* was extended out to the three-mile limit.

The Johannesburg Zoo has separate entrances for whites and non-whites. Once inside, the zoo-goers mix. They breathe the same air, laugh at the same monkeys, feed the same bears. When it is time to go they must split once more and leave by separate exits.

City buildings have separate elevators, one marked for "Whites" and another labeled "Goods and Natives." Sometimes the sign says only "Goods," but if you are black you know that elevator is for you, too.

The temptation is strong to tear down the signs or deface them. (One trick guaranteed to cause confusion is to alter a sign that reads "Non-White" by scraping off the "Non.") But in South Africa it is a serious offense to damage the signs of *apartheid*. The offender may be fined or jailed or even whipped. Besides, there are other opportunities for Africans to outsmart the whites—for example, by getting on and off forbidden white elevators, automatic ones, that is, at the second floor, where the starters cannot catch them.

Most dry cleaners are totally segregated. Some will not accept clothes from blacks at all. Others have separate counters and separate cleaning equipment so that the clothes worn by the two races will not be mixed. The employees who handle the clothes and do the cleaning work are black, but this inconsistency is ignored.

Naturally, the Africans are convinced that their clothes get inferior treatment at the segregated dry cleaners. So when an African takes a best suit or a favorite dress to be cleaned, he simply tells the attendant the garment belongs to his boss. That way it is assured of getting quality treatment on the white people's side.

EUROPEANS ONLY

NOTICE

DELIVERY BOYS AND
AFRICAN SERVANTS
ENTRANCE IN LANE

Uitgang deur Duikweg
Exit through Subway.

NIE-BLANKES | BLANKES
NON-WHITES | WHITES

WHITES
WAITING ROOM.

BLANKE
WAGKAMER.

NON-EUROPEANS & GOODS

SPOORWEG GENEESHEER
RAILWAY MEDICAL OFFICER
WHITES ONLY   NET BLANKES

EUROPEANS ONLY
SLEGS BLANKES
LADIES REST ROOM
DAMES · RUSKAMER

2ND CLASS KLAS
HALTE
STOP

BUS STOP
BUSHALTE

Z VALLEY

SLEGS VIR NIE BLANKES
NON-EUROPEANS ONLY

429

HUURMOTOR
STAANPLEK
VIR BLANKES.
TAXI RANK
FOR WHITES.

TAXI
WHITE PERSONS

GARAGE   DEL

ALL NON-EUROPEANS AND
TRADESMEN'S BOYS WITH
BICYCLES, PLEASE USE
SMAL St. ENTRANCE.
BY ORDER.

NON-EUROPEANS
TELLER
NIE BLANKE
KASSIER

BELOW SUBSISTENCE

Payday, anywhere else in the world, is the happiest of days. It's a time to smile and unbend a little with the good, confident feeling that comes of having a bit of cash on your hip. But in black South Africa payday is the worst of days. It's the time when you must settle your accounts, and always the debts amount to more than you have earned. In the midst of South Africa's abundant economy, forty-five per cent of the black families live on incomes below the subsistence level. We call it living "below the bread line," living on less than the bare-bone minimum of food, shelter, and clothing required to keep a person alive and moving. A survey made in 1959 concluded that a South African family of five needed a minimum monthly income of $77, without provision for medical care, education, furniture, or holidays. Inflation has been fierce since then, so that the minimum has gone up, but the African has only been left farther behind. His average family income is barely $50 a month.

It is not that Africans don't work. There is no famine of jobs. In fact, in the five main areas of the economy—mining, manufacturing, construction, railways, and the post office—African workers outnumber whites by three to one. The crime is that the Africans are kept artificially poor. The white establishment accomplishes this by barring Africans from all but the most menial of jobs, paying them intolerably low wages, and leaving them no recourse within the law by which to change their condition.

The color bar in industry excludes Africans from almost all skilled jobs, and thus robs them of any ambition to develop their skills. In part the color bar is a legal tactic enforced through "job reservation" laws. But mostly the bar is kept intact by individual bigotry. In many offices, shops, and factories white workers refuse to work on a par with non-whites. In trades where apprenticeship is required, such as the building industry, Africans are not taken as apprentices and thus are denied the first step essential to becoming a master carpenter, plumber, or electrician. Only when an employer is desperately short of qualified white personnel will he put a black man in a "reserved" job. Because of the shortage of skilled labor, some Africans lately have been hired to drive heavy trucks, to wait on white customers in stores, and to work as typists and bookkeepers—careers that had been considered beyond them. But always the African holding such a job gets paid less than his white counterpart, and works without any permanent tenure, no matter how long or how well he does in his work.

"The job's only temporary," the employer reminds him, "until we find somebody regular."

Should an employer try to upgrade his black workers he courts trouble. Often his white employees will revolt. Or the law may descend on him. Two directors of a construction company in Pretoria recently were convicted and fined for breaking the Industrial Conciliation Act of 1956. Their offense was to hire an African to operate a power crane on a new building project. The fact that they had tried and failed to find a white man for the job was judged no defense.

Separation salves the conscience of white South Africans. Because they live miles from the black zones and rarely venture into them, they have only fanciful ideas of what living conditions are like below the bread line. One popular myth is that Africans can live much more cheaply than whites. That's a bad joke. A saying in the township goes: "We are paid as Africans, but we have to buy as white men." Food costs no less for the African. His clothing is cheaper only if it is of poor quality. If it is, he can expect the garment to turn to rags before he has finished paying for it. The relocation housing in which more and more Africans now are living is modestly priced, but it is still far too high for people living below subsistence, who must figure that relocation means longer trips and higher rail fares to reach their jobs.

But food is the main concern. Most non-whites live in a chronic state of partial starvation. They cannot afford to buy enough of even the plainest food to properly sustain life. The result is widespread malnutrition, sickness, deformity, and death. One black infant in every four dies before its first birthday because its mother can not provide the necessary food and hygienic surroundings to keep it alive. One half of all black children die before they are sixteen.

Children in school try to concentrate while

their stomachs are aching for a simple slice of bread, the breakfast they did not have. Few working men and women eat enough to attack their manual jobs with any degree of energy or vigor. Sixty per cent of them leave home in the morning with nothing in their stomachs except a cup of tea or coffee. Eleven per cent don't even have that.

Along with hunger and disease, another sure by-product of artificial black poverty is crime. It takes only simple arithmetic to figure that if a family's income is below the bread line, and yet the family survives, it must be making up the difference somewhere. The answer too often is petty thievery: shoplifting, stealing from an employer's home or his warehouse. It is one more little irony inflicted on the white master that he must live surrounded by thieves and can trust no one. But he must ask himself, how else can his underpaid employees stay alive? Of course small, silent crime can expand, often merely by accident, into big, bloody crime. As one hard-pressed family provider told me, "When the struggle gets too savage, you must become savage, too."

One afternoon in Mamelodi, one of the large townships of Pretoria, I saw a little girl who couldn't have been more than six. She was carrying a baby sister on her back. Children caring for children is a common sight in township streets, but I watched this one, bowed under her load, wander over to a ramshackle house and hand the baby, who was crying now, over to an older girl, who looked as though she should have been at school. "What are you doing home?" I said, somewhat severely, because many children stop their schooling before they should. "I have no proper clothes for school," she said, and began to cry.

Her name was Gracie Matjila. She was ten years old. Because of her ragged condition she stayed home and "baby-sat" for her little sisters. In effect, Gracie's childhood was over.

She was crying, it turned out, because her baby sister was hungry and it reminded her that she was hungry, too. What had she had for breakfast? A drink of black tea, without milk but heavily laced with sugar. It gave her just enough energy to get through the day. She would not see another meal until evening, when her parents returned from work. Last night's porridge

bowl was still somewhere about, however, and with diligent scraping she and her brothers and sisters might be able to come up with at least a taste of something for lunch.

Block after block in the townships are cluttered with dozens of children like Gracie. By day there are almost no adults around. Just kids, looking after kids. They can be naughty, turn the house upside down, set fire to it. Who's to know? Mothers go off to work to supplement the father's income and the kids sleep in. If they fail to get up for school, the mothers don't know it.

Often parents leaving for work or older children leaving for school lock the house and take the key. That leaves the young children to play all day in the dooryard or on the street. If they survive, it isn't long before the street becomes their first home, and the house of their parents merely a temporary shelter.

On one of these streets live Daniel and Martha Mogale, a family whose plight is typical. I had known them for many years; they were good people, for whom tribal values still had meaning and whose strong ties to old ways helped hold their family unit together. Although Daniel and Martha had nine children and were desperately poor, they were still a family. How long they could remain so was a day-to-day proposition.

Daniel Mogale, the father, had worked ten years for the railways. He had started as a laborer, laying track, and had moved up to become cook and general helper to a team of white technicians who traveled the line, testing engines and other equipment. He earned $42 net a month. That was less than enough to keep the family from starving, so Martha Mogale, despite the fact that she had nine children at home, went out to work at various small jobs. Some days she would take her place in the rows of women who hawk fruit and peanuts on busy street corners. If she pushed and cajoled the passersby aggressively enough, she might come home with a few hard coins. Or she might not. Such vendors are not licensed. If the cops were feeling surly that day, Martha and the others might have to leave their wares behind and run for it to avoid being arrested.

When her second son was only four months old, Martha began working as a washerwoman in

white homes in Pretoria. For eighteen years thereafter she slung the youngest of her babies across her back early each morning and took the train to the city. At one point she was leaving home at 4:30 a.m. in order to reach her work by 6. But as Mamelodi grew and the trains became more crowded, commuting with a baby became increasingly dangerous. Caught in the rush-hour jam, Martha would plead, "Please, you are crushing my baby." The growled retort was "Then leave the baby at home." Eventually, Martha stopped trying to get into the city to work. She did find part-time duty in the township as a laundress.

Every day after school the two older Mogale boys, Henry and Daniel Jr., sold peanuts at the railway station. Their efforts added perhaps $1 a week to the family pot.

Even with so many pitching in, the Mogales often could not pay the rent on their four-room house. It amounted to only $7 a month, but sometimes they fell several months behind, and then they received frightening letters from the township superintendent of housing threatening to evict them. The house itself offered little more than bare shelter. It had no running water or electricity. The school-age children did their nightly homework by the uncertain light of a paraffin candle. Martha prepared meals on a coal stove which also provided the only heat. It was the only item of any noticeable value in the house. The furniture was crude and sparse. There was one bed. Daniel and Martha and the two youngest children slept in it. The other children slept, as well as they could, on grass mats on the floor, with old coats and sacks as blankets. Each child had the clothes he wore and little more. On washday they appeared in rags or not at all.

Every evening the Mogales played a desperate game of "what shall we eat tonight." Their staples were tea and a porridge made of corn meal. Vegetables were a luxury; usually they got by with pumpkin leaves, beet tops, and dandelion greens. Meat was served only on Sundays. Most Sundays, anyway. The first week after payday the eating might be pretty good. But as the month grew older the porridge grew thinner. While waiting for dinner, the kids one by one would fall asleep —just pass out where they sat. Each dozed off hoping to be waked up soon by the call to dinner. But sometimes their sleep lasted through the night without interruption.

Each month on payday Daniel Mogale conscientiously emptied his pay packet to meet as many outstanding accounts as he could. But he always managed to set aside a small portion of his wages for a monthly ritual of celebration. He used it to buy bakery bread as a treat for his family. One and one-half loaves for a family of eleven was the limit of what Daniel Mogale could afford.

One evening when the money squeeze was worse than usual, Daniel told Martha, "I think it would be much cheaper for you to take the kids and go to live with my mother in the tribal reserve. At least until I can get things sorted out." So, grudgingly, the family broke up. Daniel and Henry stayed on in the house, living as bachelors. Daniel worked. Henry continued in school. Martha took the others and moved in with grandmother in the reserve.

But that solution did not work for long. In the reserve the crops failed, as usual, and Daniel found he now had two homes to support. Martha was unhappy to be separated from her husband. School in the rural area was nearly ten miles away, a long hike for even the most determined scholar. The young Mogale kids stopped going.

It was Henry who proposed a way to bring the family back together. He would give up school, he said, and get a full-time job. Reluctantly his parents agreed. So at fourteen Henry Mogale, having finished not quite the equivalent of grammar school, went to work in a plastics factory. With the help of his wages, Martha and the children were able to return to the township and a semblance of family life was resumed.

Moses, the second son, was the most talented member of the Mogale family. He played an exciting jazz guitar and was a clever painter. Most importantly, he had an instant knack for electronics. He could fix anything—radios, toy trains, anything. Here, if developed, was just the aptitude that South African industry is looking for.

I have not seen the Mogale family for some time, but I have heard that Moses, too, has given up his studies. He quit after finishing only one year of high school.

Gracie Matjila, hungry and without proper clothes for school, tearfully tends her little sister.

Above: After breakfast of tea laced with sugar, Jane Mogale scrapes pot for crusts of last night's porridge, which may be her only food till evening. Women hawking fruit (right) are usually too old or too ill to work as domestics, and their profits from this are very small. Denied vendors' licenses, they often have to pick up their wares and run to escape arrest. With older children in school and mothers at work, baby baby-minders (opposite) are a common sight on African township streets.

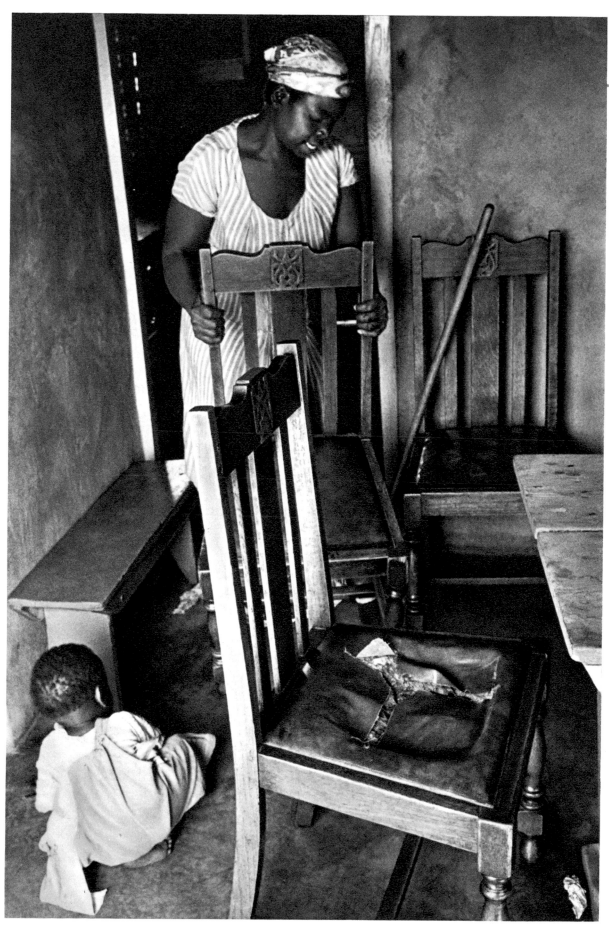

Living room furniture. Only thing of any value the Mogales have is stove bought on time.

Low-paid Africans buy high-priced goods on time in white-owned stores like this one.

Below: There is one bed in the Mogale house. Daniel and
Martha and their two youngest sleep in it; others sleep on floor.
Above: Moses Mogale does homework by candlelight.
Township houses are not equipped with electricity. Right: Infant
suffers from advanced malnutrition. Like one in every
four African children, he died before his first birthday. His
father has worked nineteen years for railways.

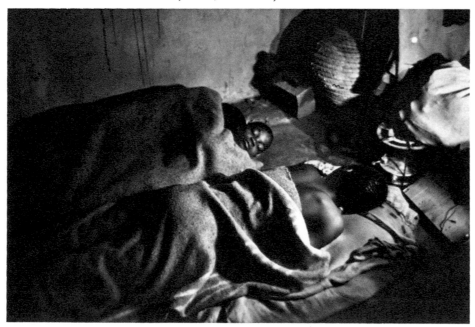

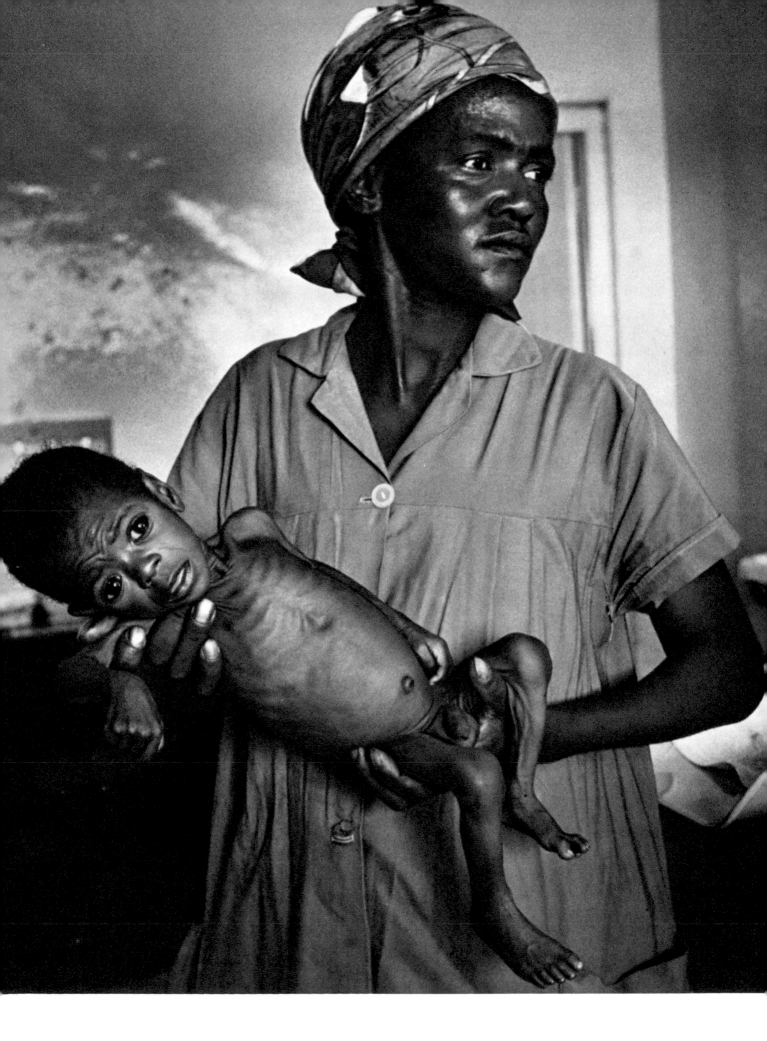

EDUCATION FOR SERVITUDE

"When I have control of native education," said Dr. Hendrik F. Verwoerd in 1953, "I will reform it so that natives will be taught from childhood to realize that equality with Europeans is not for them." Verwoerd was not yet Prime Minister, but as Minister of Native Affairs he was a figure of importance in the South African Government. He was speaking in support of the so-called Bantu Education Act, which would transfer control of African education to his department. If passed, it would give him absolute power to decide what schools could exist for Africans, who might teach in them, and what might be taught.

Under the Act, the Minister explained, the Bantu would be given no more education than he needed to perform his menial function in the South African economy.

"There is no place for him in the European community above the level of certain forms of labor," he said. "For that reason it is of no avail for him to receive a training which has as its aim absorption in the European community.... What is the use of teaching a Bantu child mathematics when it cannot use it in practice?... That's ab-surd." The child simply grows up to be an "imitation European."

The Act was passed and has been in effect for thirteen years. By now, much of what Dr. Verwoerd promised has come to pass. Each day some two million young Africans, neatly turned out in the compulsory uniform of white shirt and black pants or jumper, enter segregated Bantu schools to be educated for servitude.

Educational facilities, like everything else provided for the African, are outrageous. In Mamelodi, for instance, where many of the pictures for this chapter were taken in 1965, a population of ninety thousand is served by fourteen primary schools and one high school. You hear little complaint, however. The township appreciates its good fortune in having even that much. In some areas, the white administrators simply shrug off a large population, saying, "It's more than we can cope with," and the people have nothing. Children in this fix try to squeeze into the schools of neighboring communities, if there is any way for them to get there.

The average African student attends school

only three hours a day. Schools normally have two shifts, one beginning perhaps at 8 a.m. and the second at 11. If there is an overflow of children, as there usually is these days, one or two additional shifts will be arranged in the afternoon and special teachers called in to help carry the load. For by then the teachers who have worked the first two shifts, often facing as many as one hundred pupils at a time, are exhausted.

Faculties are understaffed, underqualified, and underpaid. Work loads are inhuman. A new school at GaRankuwa was permitted to open with only three teachers for seven hundred students.

Paradoxically, although there is an acute shortage of teachers, many of them cannot get jobs. This is because school boards budget for only so many positions and will not expand to accommodate more, even though their enrollment is grotesquely enlarged and teachers are available. I know two men with teacher's certificates who for lack of jobs are bike-riding delivery boys for a liquor store. I know another who was a messenger boy at the school where he earned his higher-primary teacher's certificate.

There may be openings far out in the country, but few people are eager for these jobs because of the hours consumed each day going to and from work. One teacher I met must rise each morning at 5 a.m. in order to be at school on time.

Unlicensed teachers, some of them as young as sixteen, are the only supplement to full-time staff. They usually are put in charge of the littlest ones, the beginners whose habits of learning are just being formed. If these girls are not very good teachers, they are at least worth their salaries, which may run as little as $14 a month. (Even this small amount is a burden on the parents, however, for extra teachers are not a budget item and must be paid for by exactions on the parents.) Since qualified teachers with years of experience may get no more than $57 a month—servant's pay—some of the young extra teachers wouldn't dream of a career in education; they are simply passing time until they enter nurse's training.

Some of the school buildings are new but all are bursting at the seams. Overflow classes may be accommodated in a church or in any empty shack that is available. Some, for which there just

is no room, do their lessons outdoors, following the shade around the school as the hot sun advances through the sky.

There is a perpetual shortage of furniture. Many schools, including new ones, have no furniture at all, not even a desk for the teacher. In winter, the scholars at empty schools bring strips of cardboard to sit on to ward off the chill of the concrete-slab floor. Where churches are pressed into service as classrooms, the need for furniture and supplies is acute, but the Government says, "We aren't required to furnish churches." At best, three or four children may have to squeeze around a two-seater desk, while an entire class huddles on benches, relics of years of hard use and slapdash repair.

Books are a precious rarity. The teacher who orders sixty primers may be allotted two.

Writing, music, and simple hygiene are among the primary subjects taught, although the schedule permits no more than twenty minutes to be devoted to each one. In such conditions learning occurs by accident, if at all. "It's impossible to hold the children's attention," one teacher told me. "In a very full class I cannot even walk through the room to get to those in the back. I would have to climb over children who are sitting on the floor and in the aisles."

A sad problem is fatigue, particularly among second-shift youngsters who are too small to walk the long route to school by themselves and must go off with older kids in the first shift. Or whose parents must go to work early and have no one to leave their children with. Accordingly, every day, the schoolyards are full of little ones playing, idling away the hours. By the time it is their turn for school they are tired and hungry and many of them fall asleep in class.

Teachers have told me that it is possible for entirely normal children to learn nothing during a school year because of weariness and languor from long hours and undernourishment.

Another problem—a divisive one—is that under Bantu education classes are taught in the tribal vernacular of each locality, even though English and Afrikaans remain the official languages of the land. This supposedly reflects the Government's concern for the maintenance of

tribal identities, but its principal effect is to reinforce the separateness of South Africa's many peoples. The tribal tongues are, of course, inadequate to the technical vocabularies of the day. This lack the Bantu Education Department has met by inventing its own vernacular terms in these areas, although they are incomprehensible to technician and tribesman alike.

Black children may begin school at the age of seven, after their parents have presented proof that they are legal residents of the township. School is not compulsory for Africans, nor is it free. A tuition fee is charged. Pencils and paper are extra. Uniforms, too. The typical hand-to-mouth African family must sacrifice to pay for even this rudimentary education of its children. Conditions at home may combine with conditions in the classroom to encourage truancy and dropping out. If there is no money for school fees or no parent at home to enforce attendance, a youngster's schooling may halt when he is nine or ten.

For most African children education ends in any case after Standard Six, the two so-called sub-standard and six standard years of primary school. A youngster is barred even from entering high school unless he has better than a "third-class pass"—that is, unless he graduates from Standard Six with better than third-class (about C-average) grades. This stiff requirement eliminates large numbers of African children who might otherwise wish to keep on with their education.

High schools are few and far between, and repeat most of the deficiencies of the lower schools. Although their enrollments are proportionally smaller, they are nonetheless crowded, as well as poorly equipped, inadequately staffed, and intellectually barren. In junior high school, courses include social studies, music, agriculture, religious education and homecraft. The final two years of high school, however, are extremely difficult for black students. After years of sub-standard preparation, and in a tribal vernacular, they are suddenly thrust into the same college-preparation course, in English, that is offered in white high schools to equip young people to take college-entrance examinations. The acceleration is too great for most black students, and only a particular, well-endowed few ever make it into college.

There are three tribal colleges for blacks, controlled by the Government, administered by whites, and located only in the Bantustan reserves. Academically, they are little better than high schools, although even at that they are short of qualified applicants. From these emerge the few black lawyers, teachers, social workers, and professional men permitted in South Africa's closed society.

Down the road, a world away, education for the white student is free, compulsory, and first class. The difference, as in so much that unjustly divides the races in South Africa, can be explained in money terms. Four and a half per cent of the national income is spent on education, but less than one-tenth of that is spent on Africans. The money spent per year for each white student ranges from R112 to R158 ($157 to $221), depending on the province. For each African pupil it is only $16.80 per head. The round comparison usually made is $14 spent on the white student for every $1.40 spent on the African. Even that ratio is getting more lopsided. While the number of African students expands, the Government for a decade has held down its contribution to black education to R13,000,000 ($18,200,000). Any further expansion and development, says the Government, must be financed by the Africans themselves.

But how? A large part of the financing of African education already is borne by the blacks. State aid is related directly to the taxes they pay, rather than to the country's general revenue. In 1961, four-fifths of the African general tax went to education. By 1964, all of what Africans paid in taxes—a sum of R7,800,000 ($10,920,000)—went to education. If new buildings and new equipment are needed, the parents themselves are required to meet the Government halfway by sharing costs, rand for rand. The money is collected in special levies over and above taxes and school fees. In the poverty-stricken townships and reserves, such money is hard to come by.

Any graphic breakdown of the African school population would take the shape of a broadly based pyramid sloping flatly to a narrow, not very tall peak. The ratio of children in primary grades to secondary grades is thirty to one. It would have

continued on page 109

98   *Earnest boy squats on haunches and strains to follow lesson in heat of packed classroom.*

Teacher above is struggling with one of her two daily sessions of one hundred students each. Children learning to write hardly have elbow room to mark their slates. Children at right must share tribal-language reader because of shortage of supplies. Principal of this school ordered sixty readers from Government, received two.

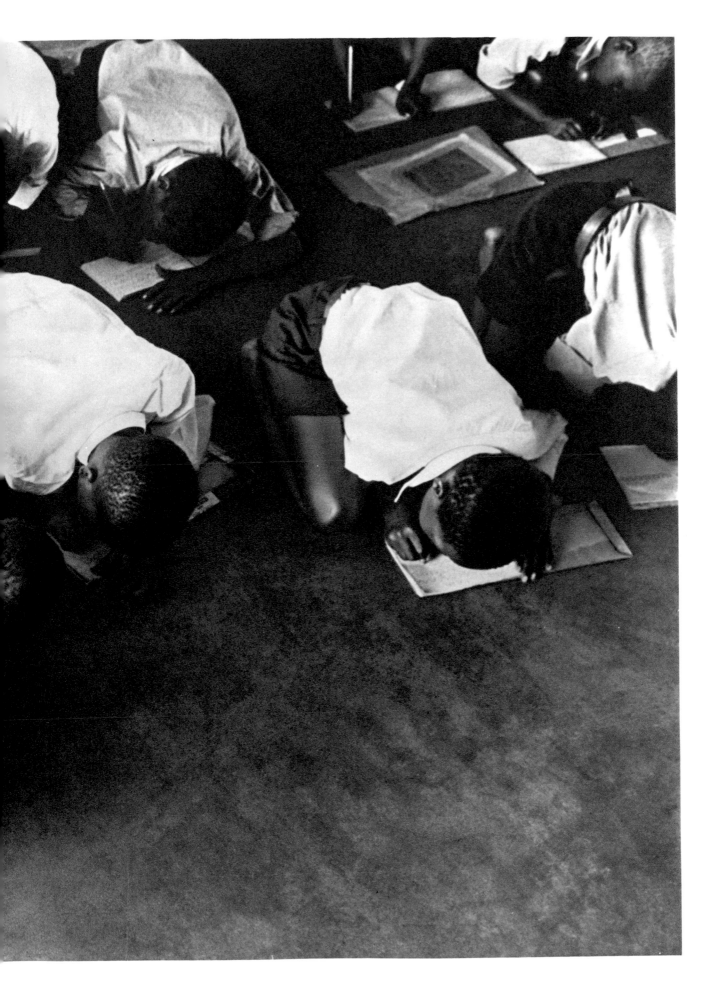

Students kneel on floor to write. Government is casual about furnishing schools for blacks.   103

*Because of the shortage of
school buildings, African children attend
classes in any available structure—
a tin shack (right) or a church (below,
right). For new school to be
built, township residents must first
raise half the cost. Below:
Brand new school, with no desks. It
opened with seven hundred
students and only three teachers
assigned by Government.
Without supervision, pupils have
gone to recess leaving
books scattered and trampled.*

Mothers seeking to enroll children for first time (above) wait in line to get essential documentary proof from superintendent's office that child is bona fide township resident. Right: Small scholars have come early to school, must wait in yard until 11 a.m. session.

By time afternoon session begins, fatigue has caught up with teacher and pupils alike. She has just finished with one overcrowded class, her children have waited three hours. Girl at board is untrained extra teacher waiting to enter nurse's course. Left: Child gives in to weariness.

to be reduced to seven to one to be considered good. Although the number of African students increases by a hundred thousand every year, the Minister of Bantu Education was able to boast, in 1964, a decade after the education act was enforced, that eighty per cent of all Africans between the ages of seven and twenty were "literate." The commissioner's standard of literacy was limited to "anyone who can read and write his own [tribal] language reasonably well, has a reasonable knowledge of the two official languages and has been provided with a basis to improve his own education." This is a meaningless criterion, considering that most high-school students today cannot compose or write a decent letter in English or Afrikaans, although in my own experience, before Bantu education, we were able to write really quite well by the end of Standard Two.

This also represents the subtle difference between discriminatory education under the British and that under the Afrikaners. The British, and the succession of pro-British Governments after Union, were not any more eager to educate the black man than the present Government, although it might have seemed that they were because they encouraged the African — and themselves — to believe that in a misty, future Someday there would be a multiracial South Africa with equality for all. Educated blacks were a token of that promise, but too many of them would have been intolerable. So there were fewer schools than there are today, and fewer children in school, although the school day ran full time and the intellectual level was higher. The Afrikaners, of course, want a South Africa in which there is no future for blacks, except in Mr. Verwoerd's terms. Thus their more widespread, but even more hopeless, education for servitude.

The Nationalist Government likes to say that blacks in South Africa get more education than they could anywhere else on the continent. If true, it yet means little. A study that traced a generation of African students through their school life unearthed these statistics: Of 211,629 African children who entered school in 1951, a mere 1,040 were still enrolled in 1963, when they all should have been finishing the twelfth grade. One survivor for every two hundred who started. Of the 1,040 who completed twelve years, only 298 passed their final examinations.

Somehow, the Government managed to warp even that forlorn figure to its advantage. The 298 Africans who successfully matriculated in 1963 represented an increase over the 246 who made it the year before. The Government happily claimed a statistical improvement in Bantu graduates of twenty-eight per cent.

Teacher toward end of her day in school.

HOSPITAL CARE

Like everything else in South Africa, medical care is segregated and unequal. For black people there are too few doctors and nurses, too few hospital beds, too few medical supplies and services. There are shortages of everything but pain and neglect.

Most Africans are treated by white doctors at public outpatient clinics in the black townships, or at one of the provincial hospitals designated for them. Everyone would go elsewhere if he could. Africans approach the clinic with reluctance, the hospital with fear. If a man has a minor ailment, he just "walks it off." Only if the trouble is so serious he can't help himself will he submit to hospitalization. If a fellow breaks his leg, for instance, his family and friends worry less about the fracture than the fact that he has to go into the hospital. This is because every African knows the ordeal that lies ahead of him when he seeks medical treatment. It is like going to prison, except that the hospital may be worse.

Hospital departments operate regularly at no better than one-fourth staff. The single doctor in charge of a clinic may see more than a hundred patients in a day that sometimes stretches to thirty hours. Obviously, these men are conscientious and dedicated. But such stress does not make for good medicine and, in any case, the doctors are too few to stem the tide of misery that engulfs them.

There are black physicians, but not many, for it takes extraordinary persistence and luck to surmount the obstacles officially put in the path of an African attempting to acquire an education in one of the professions. Until a dozen years ago white universities used to enroll and educate a small number of African medical students. But no more. Now black doctors are trained in separate schools, and to care only for non-white patients. There are pitifully few of them, but the Government refuses to subsidize additional training facilities.

It is against the laws of *apartheid* for an African doctor to minister to a white patient in a hospital, even if the patient is dying. White doctors, however, may serve either race. This point is driven home early. White medical students learning anatomy may practice dissection on both white and black cadavers, but black students are forbidden to touch a white cadaver. They may dissect only black ones.

Discrimination continues after graduation. At Baragwanath Hospital in Johannesburg, an all-black institution of more than two thousand beds, which is the largest in the southern hemisphere, the African doctor on staff receives about one third the pay his white colleague gets for the same work. The hospital swimming pool is restricted to White Staff Only. Even the hospital tearoom, where off-duty staff go to relax, is off limits. If the black doctor wants a cup of tea he must walk back to his segregated living quarters and drink alone. One African in training at Baragwanath told me, with a mixture of rage and amusement, that the moment he had graduated he was going to jump into the all-white swimming pool.

Rather than endure these constant humiliations, most black physicians go into private practice. They do quite well financially, not as a result of high fees, but because their hours are long and their case loads inhumanly heavy. In Mamelodi, for instance, there were exactly three African doctors to tend more than ninety thousand people—plus, of course, the one white doctor at the one clinic.

Because hospitals are so crowded, they will not accept a patient unless he bears a letter from his personal doctor or, more likely, a written referral from the clinic. So the African who is ailing goes first to the clinic.

People start arriving at 5:30 in the morning,

just to be first in line. To keep warm in chilly weather, they collect scraps of paper and build little fires on the ground where they stand. Inching along to the head of the line may take several days. The clinic can treat only so many at a time. After a certain hour the door is closed and no more are seen that day. It is worse for children. They are seen only on Tuesday and Friday. If your child falls ill on Tuesday after the door closes he has quite a wait ahead of him.

If the clinic doctor decides you need hospital care—and only the most imperative cases are referred—he gives you the proper papers and you arrange to transport yourself to the hospital. (In Pretoria it is twelve miles from the township.)

Now the waiting begins all over again, only the queues are slower and there are more of them to get through. At the end of the first one is an admitting doctor who must decide, after a quick look at you and your referral papers, whether you really deserve hospital treatment. Many are turned away, although they are so obviously ill that even a layman can see it. There are always some who are refused because they did not know they were supposed to have a paper from the clinic and came straight to the hospital instead.

Should the first doctor accept you, you then must stand in another line in order to open a file and have your admission papers filled out. This, too, is a long line of desperately uncomfortable people. There are pregnant mothers, feverish children, old people, workmen injured on the job. Those who are unable to stand, sit on the ground and hunch themselves along. Others sprawl in wheelchairs or on wheeled stretchers.

Once admitted, the patients are sent to have their temperatures taken. Another line. Some are directed by a doctor to have X-rays. By the time this is done and the pictures developed, the patient returns to find the doctor has *two* lines waiting for him.

Eventually the patient is assigned to a ward, and hopefully to a bed. Just getting in has taken several hours, perhaps all day. Obvious accident cases in which the victim has been struck down on the street and is rushed in by ambulance might get somewhat faster treatment. If your own people bring you in, you may be dying, but you must

wait. Some patients never live to see the end of their line.

Those who are fortunate enough to be admitted soon have reason to question their luck. The wards are so jammed that newcomers often must sleep on chairs, or on felt pads on the floor itself. The white chief administrator of one large African hospital was quoted as saying, "Natives prefer to sleep on the floor." Hardly so, although it might be true in hospitals I have seen where mattresses are blood-stained and sheets not changed between the departure of one patient and the arrival of the next. Blankets are filthy and foul-smelling. In summer the rooms crawl with vermin.

His children's ward dumps its patients together indiscriminately. Only serious cases are given beds, and several little ones may share one crib. The rest of the children sleep on the floor.

Because of the crowded conditions, wards may be swept by smallpox before it is discovered that one child has contracted it and infected the rest.

The food is meager and disgusting. Morning porridge must come from the same pot as that served to prisoners in jail. It is barely edible. I have choked it down and I know.

Nursing care is minimal, grudging, and callous. This shocks many patients, for the nurses are themselves Africans. But it is a sad business, nursing. The girls are undertrained and overworked. The preparation they get in their segregated schools is inferior to that given white nurses. They learn nothing of the psychology of nursing, nothing of human relations, nothing of the special needs of patients. They observe the doctors' brusqueness with their cases and soon learn to act the same way.

Yet nursing is one of the few professions open to African girls. It confers status and pays better than teaching or domestic service. Many girls, I am convinced, go into it for these advantages alone. Perhaps this is what makes them so unfeeling. Or perhaps there is simply so much distress they are unable to relieve that they finally become numb to it.

Actually, the reason hardly matters. For the horrors of medical care for Africans lie not in the occasional heartlessness of white doctors or the

sulkiness of dispirited nurses, but in the official policy of calculated neglect which assures that there will never be enough people or facilities to alleviate more than a fraction of the African's pain.

Even though a hospital is filled beyond capacity, some beds must be kept empty for emergency cases that arrive during the night. So at lights-out time a number of patients are taken from their beds and made to sleep on the floor beneath. The nurses believe this is less distressing to the patient than if he had to be uprooted in the middle of the night. Perhaps so, but next morning in the mix and bustle of a crowded ward, bed markings get scrambled and patients' identities become so confused that attendants don't know who is in which bed. When the doctor comes by, some patients miss their turn.

When a patient complains, he is ignored or sent home. If he insists on "escaping" before the authorities are ready to release him, he must sign an R. H. T. form—Refused Hospital Treatment. Then he is warned that no other hospital will take him. My father signed an R. H. T. while he was hospitalized with a broken hip. He told us he just couldn't take the conditions any longer. Later, when he went back to the hospital for a chest operation, from which he never recovered, he had to use a false name to get in.

My own introduction to hospitals came a few years ago when I was involved in a motorbike accident in downtown Johannesburg. The time was a few minutes after noon on a Saturday. Both my legs seemed to be broken and I could do no more than pull myself to the sidewalk and sit there. Police came to investigate. Two and a half hours later an ambulance came and picked me up. Even then the ambulance didn't go straight to a hospital. It went several more miles to pick up the victim of another traffic accident. Eventually we were taken to Johannesburg General. This hospital has two sections, for black and for white, and at that time was used mostly for emergency cases. A doctor there declared that both my knees were shattered and I would have to be admitted to a hospital. But not that one. I was left on a stretcher to "wait for transport," as they say, until another ambulance came for me. This

one took me to Baragwanath.

Once deposited at Baragwanath, I sat on my stretcher-on-wheels in a series of lines for the rest of the afternoon. The pain was pretty bad. By degrees I worked my way through the admission process. Finally, at 11 p.m., I was examined by an orthopedic surgeon. He asked about the accident and said, "We'll try to make you comfortable." He proceeded to encase both my legs in plaster up to the hip. This was to hold me until he could get around to operating on them.

That first night the stretcher I had arrived on served as my bed. The next morning I had my first food in twenty-four hours. Porridge. I decided to wait until lunch, when my family would come to visit. They brought food and for the rest of my stay I lived on sandwiches brought from home. Many other patients could not be so choosy.

The following Friday—six days after my accident—I was operated on. The orthopedic surgeons operated at Baragwanath but once a week. Altogether I was in the hospital for twenty-six days. It was long enough to educate me. Most of that time was spent in a so-called convalescent ward. The nurses had a more accurate name for it: the "dumping ward." They dumped you there and forgot you until they were ready to operate, or until you were well enough to go home. Many of the supposed convalescents in the "dumping ward" were bleeding, some dying. Some were about to be discharged with incompletely healed fractures; they would be back, with complications. A few already had come back and were again being released prematurely; they would return yet again. Dressings went unchanged for days in the "dumping ward." We helped tend each other, for we seldom saw a nurse. Doctors appeared only to discharge patients or order them prepped for surgery. The first day that I could walk again I walked out of Baragwanath.

But I went back, many times, to that hospital and to others. Sometimes I just walked in during visiting hours with my camera concealed. Other times I slipped in after hours, dodging the guards who did not want stories published about the hospital and who would stop and search anyone they suspected. From such visits I came away with the pictures for this chapter.

Young woman in pain waits her turn in emergency room of Baragwanath Hospital.

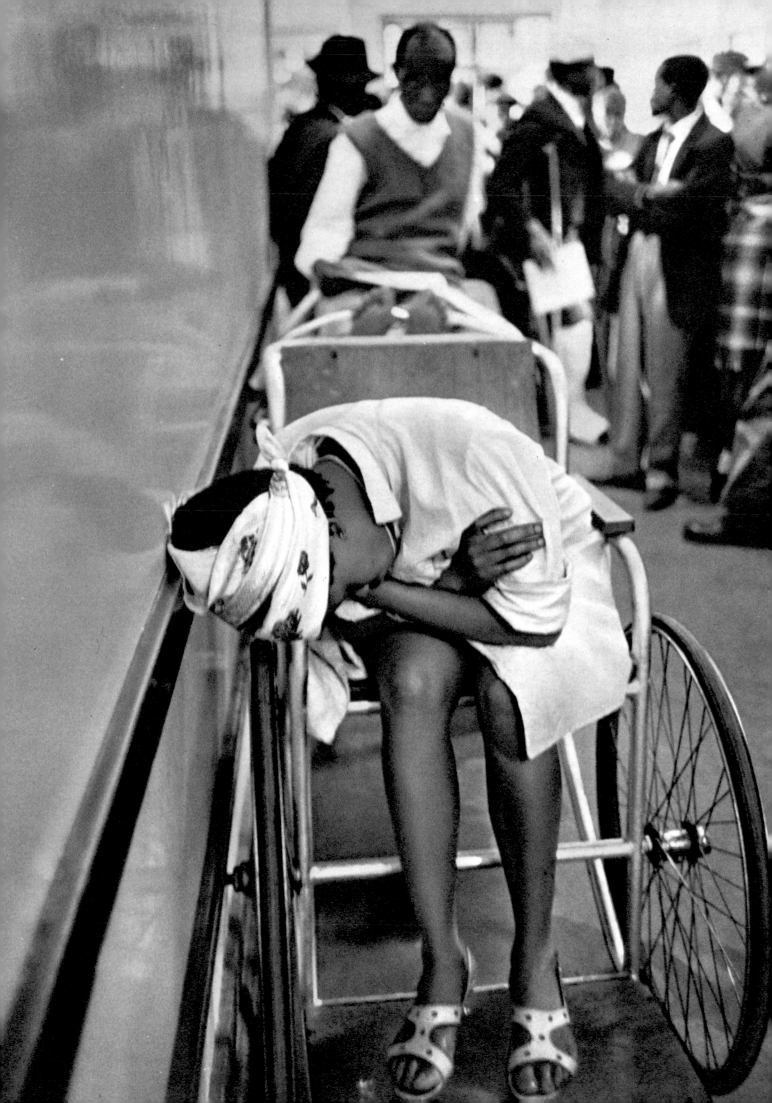

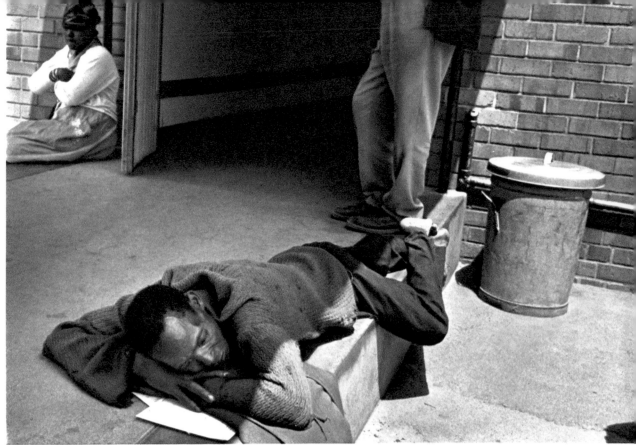

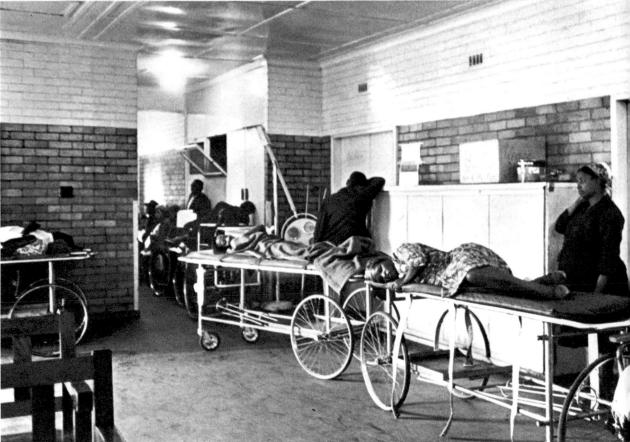

Left: The sick come early and wait in line to be
seen by doctor. Waiting and referrals can go on for a week.
Line of stretcher cases (above) from X-ray room moves
slowly through hospital. Some do not live to end of line.
Top: Patient wearied of waiting stretches out in passageway.

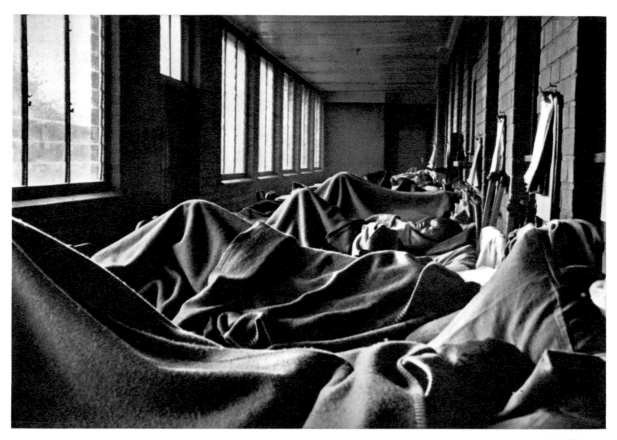

Only most urgent cases are admitted; still, wards operate at 50% beyond capacity. Patients lie on stretchers, chairs, and felt mats on floor between and under beds (following pages). Above: During day, floor patients are moved outside.

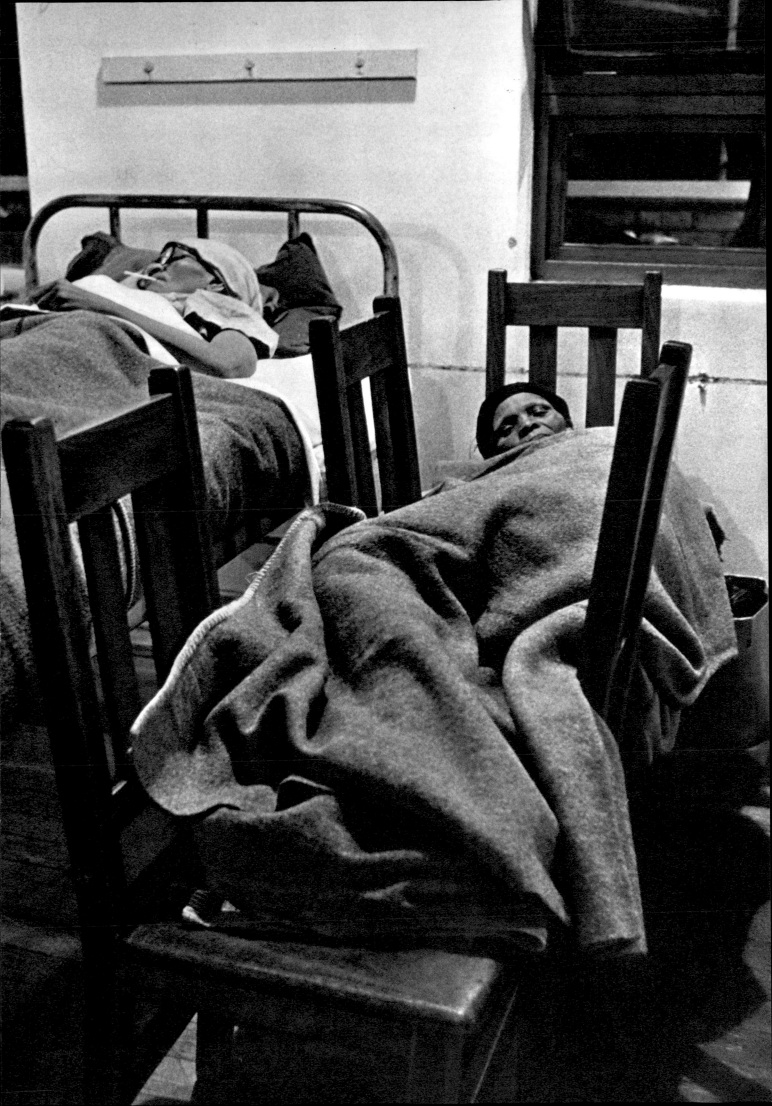

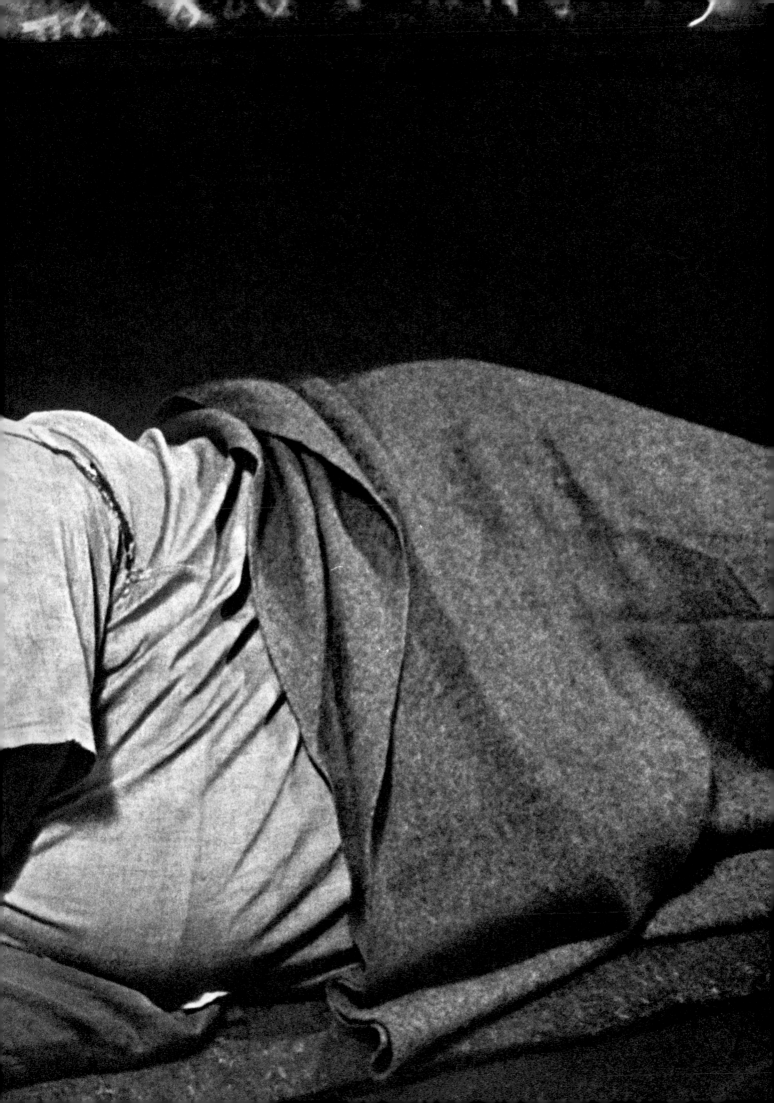

In children's ward,
patients share a corner of floor
with blankets scattered over
them. New cases have their names
written on adhesive tape stuck
to their foreheads. Infant patients
(above) must often share a bed
with two others, and spread of infectious
diseases is a common problem.
Left: Child has been judged not "serious"
enough to be given a bed.

HEIRS OF POVERTY

The streets of Johannesburg, Pretoria, and the rest are overrun with little African boys who have left home to make their own way. "City orphans" we call them. There are so many of them that they are unremarkable, commonplace, a part of the landscape. Some are as young as seven, but most are ten or twelve. They drift through the streets in small packs, like rubbish blown by a breeze. Their clothes are ragged, their bodies undernourished, and their flesh often damaged by bruises and sores. They eat what they can steal in quick, darting passes at sidewalk produce stands. And they beg from whites.

"Please, *baas*, penny. I hungry. Please, *baas*."

The effect is poorly calculated. The voice whines unattractively, the grimy little figure is repellent. Some whites reach into their pockets or purses and impersonally toss a coin or two. Others brush by. Once in a while, a choleric man will cuff a boy for displaying his misery so openly and without shame. The slap will sting, but the rebuke is meaningless. The boy simply turns away and murmurs his singsong appeal to the next white who passes by.

City orphans cut loose because their homes are hopeless. They learn early that poverty is even-handed in its cruelty. No one is spared. In Tys' home in Orlando township, outside Johannesburg, porridge was the only food ever provided, and sometimes there was not even that. Living at the edge of starvation, the fabric of the family falls apart. Fellow feeling shrivels, the heart's warmth dies out. Anyone lucky enough to acquire a penny in Tys' home spent it on food for himself —an Indian pickle or a bit of baloney to go with his porridge.

Often Tys went to school with only a cup of tea for breakfast. And since the Government had discontinued the lunch program for Africans he was distracted by hunger and light-headed with fatigue throughout the day.

At eight he quit school and took to roaming the township streets. When his mother learned of it she was upset and scolded him, invoking the all-too-real fears of the poor in South Africa. Every street child has heard the litany a hundred times and can recite it by heart:

"What is going to happen to you, child? I work every day to buy porridge for you, and you dodge school and stay out all night. What do you think your future be, without education? You'll be a loafer, working only for food and sleeping in gutters. They'll pick you up and sell you to a cruel potato farmer who will beat you to death."

Whether or not it is accompanied by slaps depends on whether it is said in anger or despair. Some few children may respond, but for most it becomes an unheard song. To escape the discord and to earn the money to support their new way of life they make their way to the city where the opportunities are more numerous and a vagabond child has the protection of being an unknown. The "outside" is rough; "There is no mother here," Tys says wisely, and he is aware that he must earn coins every day to pay for his independence. Still and all, things are better. He is ten years old now and can make his way.

The pattern of his days can be picked up at any hour of any one, for he dwells in a time continuum, without the orderly breaks and rituals that mark the lives of people living as families in houses. At 10 o'clock at night he may be found watching out for parked cars for white moviegoers. Or, if he is lucky, the car has been parked overnight and he can sleep in the back seat.

Awakened by the damp chill of dawn, he slips out to join other children in collecting waste paper and boxes for a fire to warm them till the sun is up. Mornings, those so disposed will attempt a quick wash at an untended backyard water tap. In Pretoria they may go down to the Appies River to soak some of the dirt from their

clothes. Whatever they own is on their backs; they will not change unless they can buy a new shirt or pants.

By 9 a.m., hunger pinches and they go into the open-air vegetable market to steal breakfast from the stalls, or pick over the garbage for something not too spoiled to eat, or perhaps earn a legitimate handout by doing an errand or two.

Breakfast over, the orphans—scores of them—converge on the car park adjoining, and start scuffling for cars to wash. This is their major occupation and source of income. Tys can earn a half crown or three shillings (35¢ to 42¢) per car. In the lulls between arrivals of white shoppers in their cars, the boys squat on the tarmac, smoking cigarettes and playing at dice. One watches for the police; the boys are not likely to be arrested, but they may be chased and chivvied, and anyone getting caught may be given a salutary slapping around.

After 3 p.m., car washing slacks off. Tys may take a siesta or, if he has made enough, go to an old American Western movie at a dilapidated theater serving blacks. Tys is conservative: He does not gamble and usually has a few coins secreted in the lining of his sleeve.

Or he may resume the search for food. Eating is a matter of chance for street boys. You eat when the opportunity offers. You eat when you have money. And you stop when you have none.

Evenings the boys hang about the streets. They enjoy the lighted stores. Townships are dark at night; the neon and electricity of the white cities are a novelty that never palls.

This is a good time for begging. The whites, going out to dinner or the movies, may be feeling festive enough to flip a coin to the orphans. The boys scamper about, grubby night shadows, until the city quiets down. Then, if they do not have a car to rest in, they will slip into the shrubbery of a municipal park, or behind a wall, or into some cranny they have found and go to sleep. Thus, twenty-four hours.

In a few years, Tys very likely will become a tsotsi—a tough, teen-age delinquent—living on the proceeds of thievery, assault, and any other low-grade criminal opportunity that offers. Tsotsis take their name from the U.S. zoot-suiter of a generation ago, and they act the part. They are street-corner dandies, lounging in the doorways of vacant stores, idling in the train stations and bus terminals, giving passersby the hard eye. They are the scourge of the black townships, where there is no police protection, and their own people, therefore, are the easiest and most vulnerable targets. Children on their way to the store may be robbed of the few coins they carry. Adults fear to venture out at night except in groups. Men who must work late on Fridays often prefer to wait until Monday to take their pay home, rather than risk losing it to tsotsis. For the weekend is their favorite time for robberies, muggings, and knifings. Slashed victims may be seen at the hospitals and clinics any Friday or Saturday night. The police don't care as long as whites are not attacked. "Just Kaffirs killing each other," I have heard investigating officers say. "It doesn't matter."

In his more sophisticated form, the tsotsi is bold enough to operate in white areas. Like an army recruit he has had his basic training. He is generally an accomplished mugger, thief, and pickpocket, and he is not afraid of jail. I have spent many days watching tsotsis at work.

They lived very well by stealing from black and white alike, although they preferred the white pigeon. "These whites carry money and lots of it," one young pickpocket explained. "Their pocket money is enough to pay you or me for a year in a regular job. I can't see the sense of working six days a week for a white man and have him give me an envelope [an empty pay packet]. I can steal many times as much in six seconds."

The pickpockets may operate alone or in teams. They are uncanny in their ability to spot who has money and where it is being carried. Their methods vary. One approach that works well is to walk up to a white man and chuck him insolently under the chin. People outside of South Africa have no idea how infuriated a white man can get from being touched in any way by a black. The tsotsis know that in his rage he won't even feel the wallet being lifted from his back pocket by a confederate. Another, more direct approach is the mugging shown in the pictures on pages 136-37.

It happened in broad daylight on a city street not far from the best neighborhood in a major city. White police may have been nearby, but the attack was so efficient and the group dispersed itself so quickly that there was nothing to be done.

"Stealing from whites is no sin," a successful tsotsi told me. "Whites are not going to pay you enough to live on, man. So you take it—by force if you must. We pick black pockets, too, but they usually don't have enough money to be worth it, and with us it's money first."

Pickpockets look down on lesser tsotsi. "Please don't think we're like those kids who terrorize people in the black townships," one experienced thief insisted. "They're lazy parasites, too frightened to come into the cities as we do. No gang fights for us. All we want is money, so we can live well."

It is hard not to become a tsotsi. Their easy money and relatively glamorous style of living are tempting attractions for kids still in school—kids who have few enough legitimate heroes to look up to and who will, in any case, enter a society determined to keep them subjugated.

Most tsotsis have left school, like Tys, but some have gone through the upper grades and a few have graduated from high school. No matter. The only jobs open to them are as tea-boy, or garden-boy, or messenger. White boys can drop out after the eighth grade and get a clerical job. The post office and Government departments place hundreds of Afrikaner kids in jobs every year. But an African who aspires to anything better than menial labor may turn to crime to get it.

"Now, brother," a tsotsi challenged me one day, "tell me of one African—just one—who has made it through straight wages earned from a white man." There are rich Africans: legitimately rich doctors or store owners, and illegally rich diamond and opium smugglers, shebeen kings [illicit liquor], thieves, or racketeers. But I finally had to confess that I couldn't think of a single black man who had made even a modest fortune on straight wages.

The boy who comes through his childhood and his schooling clean and manages to get a regular job is exceptional. Women tell his mother: "God is really with you. Your son is not a tsotsi."

Once started as a tsotsi, however, it is almost impossible to stop. Criminal life admittedly is dangerous, but the rewards are tempting and, anyway, what has an African got to lose? "Someday they're going to pick you up for a pass," the tsotsi shrugs, "so why not get picked up for something worthwhile."

The pass, indeed, is his stumbling block, the burnt bridge behind him. He has lived for years without one—or with a forged one, for there are many places which sell false passes, and many white men and Asians who for a price will sign your pass every month to show you work for them. But because the tsotsi is, in bureaucratic terms, unemployed, he is a vagrant and runs the risk of a two-year prison sentence if he should be picked up, or if he should attempt to get his papers in order as a preliminary step to going straight.

So he plunges deeper in, progressing if he can to the criminal elite which engages in payroll robbery.

Better than most, the tsotsi knows how to beat the system. He knows the police, too. He can spot detectives approaching a mile off. Even if it is a new plainclothesman, the tsotsi can pick him out just by his behavior. When flying squads of police launch one of their periodic clean-up drives against Africans, they rarely catch the tsotsi. It is usually the innocent bystander who gets hustled off to jail. The police note their arrests, not their ineffectiveness.

The white community has the power to deal constructively with crime, but its response is cramped by its philosophy. It cannot see delinquency and crime in terms of the poverty and despair that encourage them. It cannot even see how remarkable it is that so few Africans are, in fact, criminals.

All it understands is that "the native" is a problem. All it can see to do is to intensify the repression it already has imposed. All that is left to it to feel is fear.

For the whites, the only refuge is behind the steel bars at their windows, the only security in private watchmen and a revolver by the bedside. It is their purgatory that they must live their days in an armed camp, under a siege of their own making.

African children who have left home to fend for themselves in city streets.

Township mother fights losing battle to keep
son, age nine, from running off to live life of the streets.
She tries to assert authority with threats: "What's your
future going to be like without an education?" But it is too late;
the boy—called Papa—is out of control. Jumping
fences is something he must do well if he means to live by his wits.

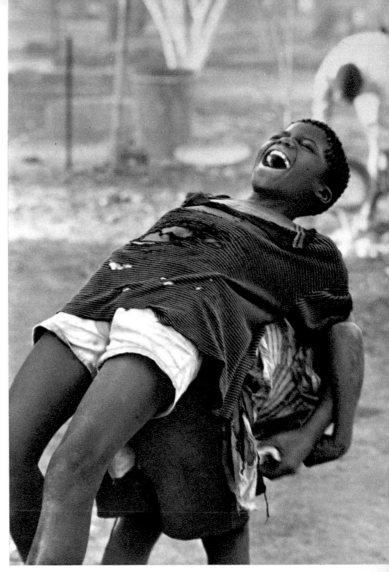

Papa with slingshot,
usual first weapon of township boy.
Line between laughing and
crying, between playing and fighting,
is very narrow for boy schooled
in the streets. He doesn't care that he
wears rags. When these pictures
were taken, Papa's mother had just
learned that he had been
playing hooky for three months.

Street boys angling for a way to eat, which they do only when they have money. Below: Their hangout at fringe of white city's lights. Opposite: "Penny, baas, please, baas, I hungry . . ." This plaint is part of nightly scene in the Golden City, as black boys beg from whites. They may be thrown a coin, or, as here, they may get slapped in the face.

Below: Tough talk and marijuana. These are
tsotsis, youths who have turned to crime rather than work as
white men's garden-boys or messengers—the usual
jobs available to young blacks. Right: A white pocket
being picked. Whites are angered if touched
by anyone black, but a black hand under the chin is enraging.
This man, distracted by his fury, does
not realize his back pocket is being rifled. Below, right: He
is allowed to go his way—till next time.

On a Saturday afternoon in heart of Johannesburg
five tsotsis mug a white man. While others watch warily, and
pretend to be passersby, fifth man surprises
victim from rear with forearm blow across throat.
As white man sags to street, second tsotsi
helps empty his pockets. Attack was over in seconds.
Gang got away with victim's weekly pay envelope.
Woman in background is scurrying out of harm's way.

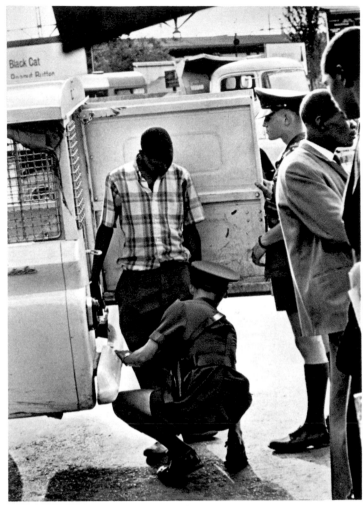

Opposite: White man assaults tsotsi who tried to snatch white woman's purse. This time black youth escaped. But others may get caught as police (left) try to solve tsotsi problem with roundups and arrests. This only toughens the youths, who take pride in being able to stand up to interrogation, beatings, and jail conditions. Below: Tsotsis are celebrating in a municipal drinking lounge— with more to spend than honest black earns in day's work.

SHEBEENS & BANTU BEER

Two kinds of drinking are found in South Africa today: legal consumption of brandy and Government-produced Bantu beer in barren, city-run beer gardens, and illegal drinking of hard liquor and strong beer in privately run hangouts called shebeens.

The shebeens came first, in reaction to the "European" prohibition against African drinking. Actually, the African's taste for drinking was well developed long before he came into contact with the white man. Drinking of homemade beer was an integral part of the religious, social, and economic life of old tribal Africa. But for the most part the African took his drinking casually. The concoctions he brewed for ceremonial use from cereal, fruit, and honey were mostly mild and rarely made him drunk.

Today the ritual significance of beer drinking has largely disappeared. But the thirst remains. For some Africans drinking is no more than a pleasant stimulant and social catalyst. But for many others, the oppressed and rootless of the cities who trudge from day to day without hope, drinking is the fast escape. It is a way for a man to unshoulder the burden of his troubles for a few hours, to drown them if he can. For such drinkers the goal is simply to "get knocked out fast." When a man prods a friend to buy a round, instead of saying, "Treat me to a drink," he says, "When are you going to make me drunk?" The name of one popular concoction is "Kill Me Quick."

With such an attitude prevailing, it is not surprising that prohibition proved no more enforceable in South Africa than it has anywhere else. While it lasted, though, it spawned a bootleg business that is still going strong years after repeal. Before prohibition, Africans had been accustomed to brewing their own beer. Women included it among their kitchen skills and a good wife took pride (she still does) in preparing a refreshing brew to soothe her tired husband.

Prohibition turned home-brewing into a profitable, if unlawful and somewhat risky, commercial enterprise. It became a handy way for a wife to augment the family income without leaving the house. Home-brewers sold to the shebeen operators, who also managed to stock their speakeasies with bonded "European" whiskey and brandy acquired, at a price, from white bootleggers. Raiding police broke up hundreds of shebeens, at least temporarily, poured a tidal wave of illicit hooch into the gutters, and arrested thousands of otherwise law-abiding Africans. But they failed to stop the drinking.

Shebeens could seldom be shut down for long. Whether serving concoctions to the poor in a backyard, or gin and brandy to middle-class blacks in a living room, the shebeens were hard to find and even harder to take by surprise. Usually they were protected by lookouts, many of them children. When raiders approached, the lookout simply tossed a stone onto the corrugated iron roof of the shebeen to sound the alarm and the evidence was disposed of at a gulp. The police could rarely determine who the guilty proprietor was; if they did know, they often could be bribed to forget it. After the all clear, the customers drifted back to finish off any liquor the raiders had overlooked.

Home-brewers learned to hide their fermenting product in ingenious, if not always hygienic, places. A common trick was to dig cylindrical holes three or four feet deep and store the brew underground in tin drums. The police countered by carrying long, slender steel bars with which to probe the earth.

The pressure of raids also stirred brewers to try to speed up their process. By adding yeast, pineapple, and sometimes old shoes and tobacco crumbs (the latter with dubious result), they accelerated the brewing—thus reducing the time when any batch was vulnerable to a raid—from a week to as little as one day.

Meanwhile, white South Africans, whose own social drinking is carried on without legal handicap, or any other noticeable restraint, professed a highly moral attitude toward African drinking. Under the guise of "protecting the native from himself," they voiced disapproval of the admittedly shabby and loosely run shebeens, where the old tribal etiquette of separate drinking for men and women was violated, where pickups could be arranged, and children were idle spectators of their parents' behavior.

Yet once South Africa began having difficulty selling its alcoholic products abroad (particularly following its break with the Commonwealth over *apartheid*), and once the liquor industry recognized the market potential of the thousands of Africans who continued to drink, even at the risk of arrest, the lure of profit to be made by legalizing liquor overcame its lofty moral stance.

Beginning in 1938, South Africa's white-run municipal governments plunged into the beer business. City-run breweries, using old tribal recipes much like the ones that had been forbidden for home use, began producing vast quantities of so-called Bantu beer. It is a thick, sour-tasting drink, purplish in color, and containing only a piddling two per cent of alcohol. The beer comes in waxed half-gallon cartons that look like milk containers. (Bottles are not used because they might explode; the brew is still fermenting when it reaches the consumer.) The city governments sell the beer at city-run beer parlors for roughly fourteen cents a half-gallon. Africans buy nearly one hundred million gallons of Bantu beer a year and the returns to the Government are handsome. In Johannesburg alone, municipal beer sales surpassed $8,000,000 in 1965, yielding a profit of $3,100,000.

The cities use their profits to pay for the limited welfare programs they conduct for the African, thus sparing white taxpayers much of the burden of providing for the poor of the community.

The city fathers proudly assert the food content of their beer. They say that half a gallon provides two-fifths of an adult's daily protein requirement. Some whites believe Bantu beer is good for ulcers and drink it for its medicinal value. But because of its acid taste, no white

market for Bantu beer has ever really developed.

Whatever its nutritional or medicinal qualities, Bantu beer is not much fun to drink. The city beer gardens where it is sold are little more than concrete courtyards with benches. They are sterile places, too brightly lit and too well-policed for comfort, where little in the way of social exuberance can be generated. Indeed, the Government-proprietor wants nothing of that kind to develop. No women are allowed, although they may buy beer from a tap outside. Singing and dancing are discouraged, and if a fellow should feel moved to strum his guitar, he may find himself ejected for disturbing the peace.

Prohibition on hard liquor ended in 1962. Since then, Africans over eighteen have been permitted to buy liquor and beer-to-go in bottle stores. There now are bar-lounges, as well, where an African can buy liquor by the drink. Like the beer business, these bottle stores and lounges for Africans are a Government monopoly. Similar places in white neighborhoods are privately owned by whites. But no African can get a license to run one.

Despite the end of prohibition and the appearance of Government-sanctioned drinking establishments, the urban African still takes much of his business to his favorite, unlicensed, illegal, friendly neighborhood shebeen. It may be the traditional backyard spot, or an elegant, dimly lit room where a wealthier clientele can listen to stereo jazz. In either place, the attraction is the atmosphere. He pays more for his drink, but his credit is good. He can drink all week "on the tick" and settle up on payday, a convenience not offered by the city beer halls. And the shebeen operates at his convenience. If it is closed when he arrives, it will open, and it will not close again until he leaves, or passes out.

Mostly it is the feeling that this is his sanctuary, a place where he isn't feeding the Government coffers every time he buys a drink, a place where he can sit at ease among his own kind and talk, drink, and be himself. The threat of a raid continues, but it is worth the risk. Home is just over the back fence and the beer keeps flowing far into the night. If a man can't drown his troubles away, at least he can make them float for a while.

Until the Government went into the business of
selling liquor to Africans, it was illegal for them to drink.
They did drink, however, in places called shebeens,
where many still prefer to gather. Above: In a shebeen, oil can
containing potent liquor is passed from man to man; jokingly
they call it "crude oil." Opposite: Expressive
face of woman denizen of the shebeens. Some men and women
stay in shebeens all day, drinking themselves witless.

Atmosphere of the shebeens is free, in contrast to that of regimented Government beer halls. When spirits run high, someone usually provides music, and a woman may break into a dance or staccato of swearwords. It used to be a social disgrace for an African woman to be found drinking with men. Shebeens have changed this.

Above: Man in shebeen tries age-old persuasion of drink
and talk on his attractive companion. Below, left: Usual way to
hide liquor from police is in four-gallon cans buried
in ground. Below: After a few drinks, young mother begins to sag.

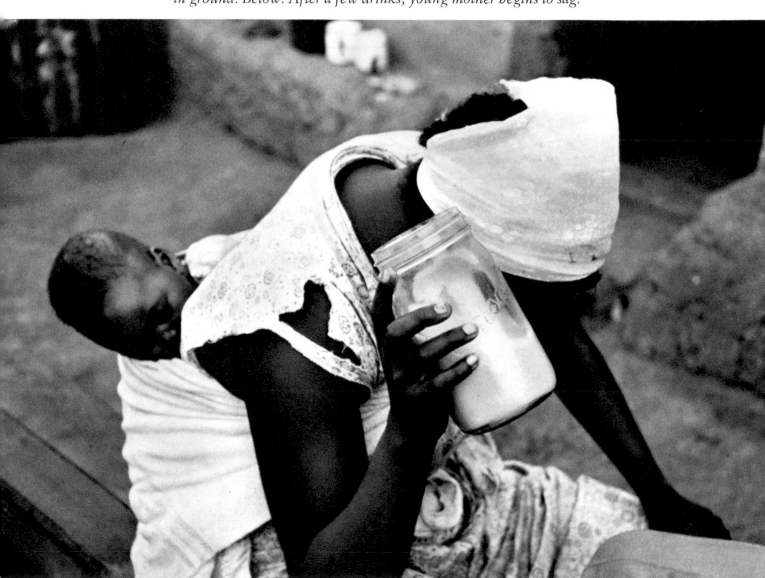

*Bantu beer: Municipalities
legally monopolize production and
sale of this brew; profits
are high. In Government beer
halls (where women are
not allowed), it is dispensed
automatically from huge
vats; in city bottle stores,
it is sold in closed
cartons. Africans may not
drink in city bars, but
may buy beer to drink on sidewalk.
Below: Friday afternoon
outside the bottle store, after
most of crowd have left.*

THE CONSOLATION OF RELIGION

Christianity's mission to South Africa has been a schizoid experience. Thanks to one hundred and fifty years of zealous missionary work, seven Africans in every ten profess the Christian faith. Of the white citizens, ninety-four per cent are Christian.

But such figures must be scrutinized. Probably nowhere on earth is Christianity so at odds with itself and pursued in so many contrasting ways. In the name of Christianity every kind of worship, from sixteenth-century Calvinism to neo-magical faith healing, is practiced. In the name of Christianity, *apartheid* is rationalized and defended. Likewise in its name, *apartheid* is condemned.

From the start, Christianity in South Africa has stumbled over the color line. Long before Government *apartheid* came into force, missionaries dispatched from Europe and the United States were preaching separation within the church. In any mixed congregation, their argument went, white members would control all the positions of responsibility. The only way the new African Christian could fully express himself would be within an all-black congregation. For that reason, and others, segregation still flourishes in orthodox Christianity today, the degree depending on the denomination and the individual church.

The extreme position, and unfortunately a most influential one, is held by the Dutch Reformed Churches. The Dutch Church teaches *apartheid* as an integral part of Christianity. Its Golden Rule is that there is no equality between black and white in church or state. The early Boer settlers brought with them a Calvinist belief in predestination—that salvation cannot be earned by good works but is limited to the "elect" of God. They were the elect, and they thought of God not as a Spirit of Unity but as the Great Divider. Cut off from the waves of humanitarianism and liberalism that have so greatly influenced the rest of the Christian world in the past two centuries, the Boers developed their own theology. The Bible was their cornerstone and as they trekked into the lonely wilderness they came to see themselves, like the Patriarchs of the Old Testament, as the chosen people. The Old Testa-

ment told them that the dark-skinned people they encountered were inferior in the sight of God. Their view of predestination convinced them that this inferiority was unchangeable. Thus the Boer held himself to be the protector of the pure faith, exercising a God-given right to rule. The black man is fit only and forever to be the biblical "hewer of wood and drawer of water."

This is the Christian message which the prime minister, almost all the cabinet officers, ninety-five per cent of the Nationalist majority in Parliament, and most of the Afrikaner population adhere to today.

Not surprisingly, the Dutch Reformed Church maintains separate churches for the different races. But they are not alone. *Net Vir Blankes* is figuratively written on many a South African church door, not all of them Boer. Whatever denomination he joins, the African can expect discrimination in some form, though it may not be as bluntly put as in this story, which made the rounds in Johannesburg a few years ago: A white man arriving early at church one Sunday discovered a black man down on his knees in front of the altar. "What are you doing there?" the Afrikaner demanded. "Just scrubbing the floor, *baas*," the black man replied.

"All right," said the white man. "But God help you if I catch you praying."

Besides segregation by congregation, the African Christian must grapple with other problems that tend to confuse him and undermine his faith. Religion anywhere is intermingled with a way of life. The white missionaries, no matter how high their purpose, could not help but impose their own Western background onto African converts whose traditions and culture were far different. To clear the way for Christianity the missionaries destroyed the culture they found without stopping to examine it. There must have been some good in the old tribal ways for them to have lasted as long as they did, but the missionaries decreed that everything African was "pagan." An African who heard the Christian message and wished to be saved had to give up— or at least appear to give up—his tribal traditions and customs. If the missionary said the sight of

bare-breasted, bare-legged women was evil, so be it. Cover them up even though the sight had never bothered the African.

In place of their old ways, Africans were instructed in the ways of a white God who ruled a world where all men are brothers, where love triumphed, and where the faithful were rewarded in the next world for their suffering in this one. Nineteenth-century English missionaries spread the gospel that "everyone is equal in Christ" and agitated successfully for the abolition of slavery. This the Boers could not forgive and still have not forgiven. But for the Africans it was a consoling philosophy and it attracted them to the mission churches in great numbers. At its best, in fact, the Christian church has acted as a mellowing influence in African life. Whatever inequalities exist in the harsh, everyday world, the African believed he would find shelter from them inside the church.

Perhaps the Africans expected too much. When their hopes were not fulfilled, resentment and disillusionment set in. Though the quantity of African conversion stayed high, the quality suffered. The proximity of large numbers of typical white Christians was probably as much to blame for this as anything. The Africans learned from white example that Christianity can be treated as little more than a religious social club, something to join because it is somehow better to be inside the club than outside, but not something to affect one's everyday life deeply.

Today's black Christian wonders why his church remains so quiet on the subject of *apartheid*. Sunday preachers generalize about social justice, but they rarely bear down on the specific injustices their parishioners suffer day after day.

The African is taught to love his brother and to pray for his enemy instead of fighting him. But he wonders who is his brother? Is it the white churchgoer? And is he being taught the same lesson?

Because they cannot find satisfactory answers to questions like these, many Africans have grown cynical of Christianity. Where, they ask, is it written that the African must take his oppression on his knees? Where is it written that the African cannot rise up against his oppressors? Instead, the church tells the African not to break the laws of the state, no matter how unjust they are, and adds the insult of including a prayer for the detested Government in its services. "Religion," the educated African sneers, "is just the white man's way of taming you." And in increasing numbers he gives up churchgoing altogether.

Many more Africans, especially the poor and the poorly educated, merely give up "white man's religion." They turn instead to other forms of worship which they find more gratifying. There are three categories of these: 1) the Ethiopian movement, 2) the Zionists, and 3) the return to ancestor worship.

From almost the earliest days, Christianity in South Africa has been splintered and fiercely competitive. One authority called it the most "overdenominationalized" place on earth. At the height of the missionary era, fifty different organizations were engaged in recruiting African members. By 1892 the African Christians themselves began to break off into independent churches. The main problem, even then, was color. The white mission clergy were slow to raise their converts to positions of authority. Those few whom they ordained into the clergy were often treated as mere "priest-boys." Inevitably, the "priest-boys" wanted their own churches and the fastest way to get one was to break with the mission authority and set up one's own congregation. These new, all-black, independent Christian churches were greatly influenced by the mission churches from which they sprang. But they refused allegiance to any European source of authority. Instead, they espoused the Ethiopian line which, at its simplest, is Africa for the Africans.

A few years later came a new and colorful offshoot of Christianity, called Zionism. African Zionism has no connection with any modern Jewish movement. It is based on a Christian sect founded on the shores of Lake Michigan in 1896 by John Alexander Doxie. By 1904, missionaries from Zion, Illinois, were carrying Doxie's teachings to a receptive African audience. Chief among its doctrines were divine healing, purification through immersion, and the nearness at hand of

the Second Coming.

As orthodox Christian influence has slipped, these independent and Zionist churches have multiplied. Today there are several thousand of them with a total membership in the millions. Each congregation revolves around a single strong leader. To the African, his church leader or "prophet" is many things. As a chief he represents the stability of the old tribal authority. As an independent minister he is a direct messenger of God. To some he is even divine. Zionist prophets in particular are believed by their followers to be invested by the Holy Spirit with a supernatural power to heal. How attractive this emphasis on healing is to the Africans cannot be overstated. Their search for good health is endless, and often you will hear this simple expression of faith: "I was ill. The Zionists prayed for me and now I am well."

As a synthesis of the old ways and the new, Zionism offers the African many pluses. If a man is ill and the white man's medicine does not help him, he may go to see the unlicensed tribal doctor without offending his church. The services themselves are loud and emotional, with a heavy dose of ritual. The congregation participates by shouting responses and singing hymns. Within his congregation the African can reestablish the feeling of community and common interest that he may have lost in the rootless and complex life of the cities.

A Zionist baptism can be an exciting outing for all concerned. The candidate for baptism is escorted waist-deep into a river and held there by the prophet or one of his assistants. Before he is immersed, the new member must make a public confession. He tells his sins and the man holding him repeats each one at the top of his lungs to the congregation gathered on the bank, listening intently. Confession and immersion are believed to cleanse and purify the candidate, and he is warned that if he does not tell all, he will surely drown. Occasionally, someone does drown during the ceremony and no one tries to help him. It is considered an act of God.

Where splintering once meant the breaking away of black preachers from white-run mission churches, it now takes the form of young blacks breaking off from established black churches. A gifted, ambitious young African who, because of his color, can't hope to reach the top in government or business can exercise his drive for leadership by forming his own church. Little formal education or preparation is necessary. In the separatist churches "good character" is deemed a requisite for a minister. Zionist prophets are expected to have "divine inspiration" as well.

The competition for primacy is strong. Sometimes the aged head of a flock has only a meager education and can read little more than his Bible. A bright young man in his congregation, more enlightened and perhaps better educated, even in African terms, may begin to interest people with ideas of his own. Eventually either the old leader or the new one must leave and begin anew. Sometimes a new leader will start with only his wife and two or three others in his flock. The growth of the sect will depend on his own dynamism. One Zionist leader has built a following of 150,000 followers.

The leaders of very small sects usually must have other jobs to get by. They may work in offices on weekdays as messenger boys or cleaning boys. But in most congregations the faithful contribute openhandedly to their leader's support. In fact, the members take competitive pride in the worldly possessions of their clergy. This contrasts sharply with the African's view of the orthodox Christian churches as money-grubbers. Many blacks have come to regard mission Christianity as a commercial enterprise first, a soul-saver second. The complaint is heard in the townships that "the Church won't do anything for you, won't even bury your dead, unless you are up to date in your dues." The white clergyman is regarded like the tax collector, as someone who shows up once a quarter to give out communion and rake in the collection. Then he goes away.

Probably because they are glad to see at least one of their own kind get ahead, the faithful take vicarious satisfaction in the opulent living practiced by the more notorious black clergy. A prime example is Edward Lekganyane, a self-styled Zionist bishop, called "King" by his followers, who has built a Mecca for his flock at

Moria City in the northern Transvaal. Three times each year they come, by the tens of thousands, on regular pilgrimage. For three days they dance, sing, eat, pray, and pay subscription money as homage to the "King." Lekganyane controls all the money himself. A millionaire by now, he delights his followers by showing off his motorized royal caravan of some fifteen luxury automobiles. Among them is a huge touring bus, a "house on wheels," which has several bedrooms, showers, a completely equipped kitchen, a speaking platform, and a built-in garage in which a minicar can ride piggyback. When he appears in public, the "King" sports two diamond rings, five fountain pens, and a gold-threaded tie worn over a stomach that plainly has never known a hungry day.

Before Christianity came to Africa, people believed that the spirits of their ancestors controlled their daily lives. There was a central god, who was called "the great, great one," or "old, old one." The departed ancestors were arrayed around him, much as the saints of Christianity are believed to be arrayed in the heavenly court. If a person looked after his ancestors well, respected them, prayed to them, and occasionally sacrificed a goat to them, it was believed that they would look favorably upon the living and protect them. But if the ancestors were neglected or displeased, then illness, misfortune, and even death would visit the kraal (tribal village). When this happened, new sacrifices had to be made to restore health, happiness, and harmony.

All this has more than historical interest because many thousands of South Africans still worship their ancestors in the old way. Thousands more, though they profess some form of Christianity, retain their belief in the power of the departed ones and turn to them, particularly in times of stress.

Ancestors are thought to reveal their displeasure through illness, drought, fever, bad luck, and a hundred other misfortunes of daily life. To overcome these negations and bask once again in the benign favor of the spirits, an afflicted person may consult any of several kinds of medicine man. The temptation is to call these practitioners witch doctors, but they object strenuously to this, insisting that their role is to heal, not bewitch. Witchcraft and sorcery are black magic.

First of three general categories of medicine man is that of Rainmaker, a function that always has been considered vital in rural Africa's crop-and-cattle economy, which is perpetually endangered by a shortage of rainfall. Second is the Herbalist, a sort of general practitioner who handles routine disturbances, such as contention in a family, money worries, and minor illness—including what white hospitals call "Kaffir poison," a physical and psychological malaise that resists Western-style treatment. The nature of the complaint is disclosed in the random pattern of bones, shells, and other magic paraphernalia thrown on the floor. The Herbalist's art is hereditary and accomplishes its cures through herbs, roots, and other primitive, natural medicines.

If the bones indicate that the patient suffers a tormented spirit, such as Western medicine might diagnose as requiring psychiatric treatment, the case is beyond the Herbalist's competence and he passes it on to the third and most potent category, the diviner.

Many of the diviners are women; their therapy for patients afflicted by an ancestor is to make them a vessel for possession by the spirit through a purification rite involving ablutions, vomiting, and sacrifices. For as long as necessary, perhaps several months, the initiate lives in the house of the diviner. When the initiate has been cleansed, the ancestor signifies approval by entering the body, thereby giving the person the ability to locate, or "divine," hidden objects. This is more than a vaudeville trick, for the diviner frequently uses his, or her, art to combat black magic—particularly to locate the poisons and other malignancies used by sorcerers to cast spells and distress people—or their cattle—with evil.

The most powerful revelation of ancestral spirits takes place in the initiation of a new diviner. The ceremony is a spectacular combination of magic and religion. I photographed one initiation in the backyard of a diviner's house in Mamelodi township. The candidate was a girl in her late teens who had turned up at the

diviner's house one day three months earlier, showing symptoms of mental illness. Since then she had lived with the diviner, an obese old woman with a big following in the township. The girl had prepared herself for initiation by undergoing a daily purification rite that featured ablution in a nearby river and self-induced vomiting. Now she was deemed ready.

The initiation began with the sacrifice of a goat to the ancestors. This alone was almost more than I could stomach. The girl went to her knees and drank blood escaping from the goat's freshly slit throat. She vomited, then launched into a wild demonstration of singing and dancing, punctuated by more vomiting.

During an intermission, while the girl rested inside the house, the old diviner challenged me to test the powers of her novitiate. The bladder of the butchered goat had been tied to a stick, and I dispatched my cousin, who had come with me, to hide the thing. When the second stage began the girl worked herself into a trance. While on her knees in the dust she began to describe aloud the roundabout route taken by my cousin, tracing him right to the backyard, about a mile away, where even then he was hiding the bladder in a tree, as I had instructed him. Urged on by the diviner, the girl got up, went to the distant yard, and fetched the stick and bladder in her hands. The crowd watching the ceremony greeted her triumphant return with joy. There was cheering and congratulations all around. For my part, it seemed an authentic divination. I could swear that no one had followed my cousin and tipped the girl off. But more importantly—and the reason the onlookers were so happy—the girl had successfully passed her initiation, which meant that through possession she was at peace with her ancestors and would henceforth be able to help and heal others.

One branch of Christianity that continues to make substantial numerical gains in South Africa is the Roman Catholic Church. The Catholics push hard on a grass-roots recruiting program. The priest in my own township increased his congregation from two thousand to six thousand in about five years.

One reason for the Catholics' success is that they preach nonracialism. Although many white Catholic laymen are among the most conservative in the community, Africans are welcome in the city cathedrals and some also attend mixed parish churches. The old Catholic reputation for conducting good schools still earns it new members, as well. African parents are desperate to get the quality education for their children that the parochial schools offer. In most cases, the children enrolled in these schools turn Catholic, if they were not already. This often sets up a conflict at home, since kids are taught that the tribal ways of their non-Catholic parents are "pagan."

Still other converts are Protestants who have quit their churches for various reasons. The criticism most often heard is that the Protestant missions are interested only in collecting money.

The Catholics have their own problems, however. Their schools and seminaries have always been segregated. Until recent years, most orders of priests and nuns were closed to Africans. It is also said that Catholic hospitals and schools are directed primarily at serving the well-to-do white communities, where the students and patients—Catholic or not—can afford the stiff tuition costs and room fees.

Catholicism tries to get its converts to observe the laws of the Church strictly in their daily life, and to cut off entirely from familiar and lifelong customs and beliefs. But many of the converts are simple, uneducated people who are attracted by the trappings of the new religion and follow it blindly—for a while. They join easily and as easily drift away. Try as he might, the priest doesn't really get through to them. While the church concentrates on preparing souls for heaven, the African has difficulty looking beyond his next meal. When his child is sick or he feels so oppressed that he is sure his enemies have put a curse on him, it is to the medicine man that he goes.

At the township level I have observed a number of young priests and ministers who realize that the Christian church must roll up its cassock sleeves and work directly to improve the lot of the people in this life, as well as the next, in the earthly houses of God as well as in heaven.

Zionist preacher delivers sermon. Deafening volume is sign of inspiration by Holy Spirit.

*Drummer intones
hymn and congregation takes it
up with gusto, swaying
bodies as they sing. Soon
they are carried away
with emotion and begin dancing
in rhythm with the drum.
Right: Man goes into a trance.
He has received the Spirit
and begins to "speak in tongues."
Sermons and prayers
follow, leading toward healing
ceremony, which is
central act of the service.*

At healing service, sick are called
forward as others move in procession around
prophet. He shuts his eyes, begins
to pray; then he seizes one of the sick,
shakes her and slaps her chest,
calling on demon to depart. Right: During
baptism by immersion, preacher
tells woman she will drown if she has
not confessed all her sins.
Another woman (bottom) is led from
baptismal rite. Zionists receive
baptism repeatedly to benefit from its
healing and purifying powers.

This Zionist pastor—
head of a tiny splinter church—
is preaching to his
entire flock in outdoor chapel.

Zionist pilgrims crowd street to
cheer Bishop Lekgunyane (in naval uniform)
as he leads procession through
Moria, the Mecca of his church. They travel
here yearly to pray, celebrate, and
make their donations of money. Below: They
inspect one result of their support:
the bishop's newly-acquired mobile home.
Bottom: A woman sips soda and eats
dry bread after her trek to Moria. She is one of
50,000 who come to three-day festival.

Children trot after Catholic missionary on his rounds in Mamelodi. People seek his help in problems other than spiritual. Opposite: Tribal convert, mystified by matter of bureaucratic procedure, comes to "Father" for an explanation. Right: Bishop in mitre makes his yearly visit to Mamelodi parish.

Priest gives Communion to sick woman.
He is among few whites who experience first-hand
the living conditions of Africans in
townships. Catholic Church's role largely
remains the traditional one of
preparing souls for eternity. Below: Initiation
ceremony of girl diviner. She drinks
blood of sacrificial goat as part of purification
rite to prepare her for
possession by ancestral spirit.

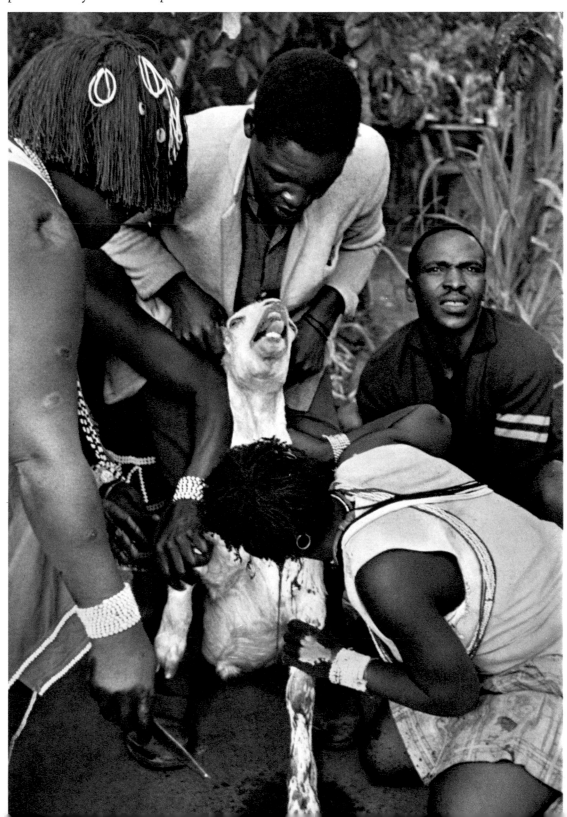

Above: Diviner studies bones to see what spirit desires for the initiate (left). Right: Possession ceremony of initiate (girl wearing strands of beads) may involve days or months of ritual dancing and singing to beat of sacred drum until irresistible force of spirit enters girl.

167

AFRICAN MIDDLE CLASS

At the peak of the black population structure of South Africa there is a relatively privileged group which can be called middle class. Exactly how many it numbers I cannot say. Probably not more than a few thousand. It contains those fortunate enough to have one of the few vocations which offer a black man the chance to earn a moderate income, and a somewhat larger intellectual elite distinguished by a high school or college education—and an aptitude for speaking English.

The economically well-endowed include doctors, lawyers, merchants, storekeepers, and most likely some shebeen owners and other operators on, or over, the edge of the law. Compared to the bottom layers of black society, they are wealthy, though not by the standards of the European and American middle classes. The marks of their success are modest: a better home than the Government-built matchboxes of the townships and on a better plot of land, a car—sometimes an expensive one, decent clothes, a glow of health and well-being that comes from adequate diet.

The educated usually have little enough to show for their achievement. Teachers, even at the professorial level, are poorly paid. So are social workers. So are those lawyers whose practice is confined to clients in the poverty-ridden townships. Thus there are many accomplished men and women whose clothes are in tatters. Yet in South Africa's discriminatory society, possession of special educational qualifications is as important as money in setting a man apart from, or above, the millions of menial laborers and rural agriculturists who are the depressed majority.

Taken together, the moneyed and the educated are the only Africans who have in any measure risen above the degradation imposed by the white community. Other blacks see their small triumphs as the only hope of escape from systematic repression. Whites view them with hatred as a threat to their supremacy.

These advantaged ones exist through a combination of circumstances. Some professional men are needed to handle the legal and medical problems of blacks that whites are loath to mix in. Someone must teach African children the shabby rudiments of Bantu Education. Merchants and storekeepers inevitably flourish through their control of the meager trade of black customers. Shebeen owners profit on the forgetfulness sold with their brew.

Some families have inherited old tribal wealth. Others are the descendants of mission-trained Africans and have known education and middle-class values for three or four generations. Among individual men and women in their forties and fifties there are many beneficiaries of the slightly more relaxed policies of an earlier time. The most onerous repressions, after all, are only a

generation old. These people can still exert the force of intelligence sharpened in the days before higher education for blacks was cut back.

And finally there is the tenacity of human spirits which will not be downed. This may sound overly emotional, but it is so. For people who have nothing, the drive to achieve something can be so all-consuming as to be almost irresistible. The obstacles placed in the path of education and opportunity and self-realization for the black man are so difficult and disheartening that many people find themselves fighting to overcome them. The situation is so miserable that there is nothing else to do, so hopeless that one is bound to win something. This is how penniless washerwomen accumulate the pennies to send a youngster to college, how a deprived and uncultivated child proves able to bring forth an artistic talent, how a man shackled by restrictions manages to teach or heal or inspirit others.

The whites do not understand this. They continue stubbornly to claim that they know the African better than he knows himself, but they do not. Whites have no idea how the African thinks or feels, or what he wants from life or to what degree he will work to get it. The white *baas,* with his unswerving belief in predestination, acknowledges no levels or distinctions among Africans. He has carried only one image around with him all his life—that of the docile native, the submissive, ignorant, obsequious black. Whether you have made yourself a doctor or lawyer or college professor, to him you are still a "semiliterate barbarian" and called only by the derogatory terms "Kaffir" or "Bantu."

When he encounters independence or ambition in a black man he is surprised and offended. To attempt to improve oneself is simply being uppity, a form of misbehavior. "What right have you got to rise up?" he asks irritably. It is as though he has uncovered a strain of nippiness in an otherwise satisfactory breed of dog. He prefers things uncomplicated and unchanged. "Give me the raw Kaffir, anytime," he says.

It is hard to avoid the feeling that white men fear any evidence of African intelligence. Certainly they ridicule and belittle it—as in the joke Africans tell about the white *baas* and his black

assistant who were planting a tall flagpole. As the African holds the pole in place, the *baas* orders: "Boy, climb up to the top and lower a tape so we can measure how long the pole is."

"Wouldn't it be easier," the African suggests, "just to lay the pole on the ground and measure it that way?"

"Kaffir," says the *baas,* "don't try to be so clever. I want to know the height, not the length."

This bitter humor of frustration illustrates the plight of clever Africans. Whatever their abilities, there is no recognition of them in the white world of South Africa. Among themselves, the skills and advantages they have acquired, whether by effort, by circumstance, or by luck, confer status and respectability. And however precarious these may be, Africans consider them worth striving for, retaining, and passing on in any way possible to their children. To this extent their example is an encouragement to blacks lower down on the social scale.

Unfortunately, the possibilities of progress for upper-level Africans are so severely limited that ambitions become distorted and growth takes strange forms. The drive for individual status becomes so passionate that there is no heart for the nobler cause of helping to improve the lot of all Africans. "Do not live above your people," urges the National Council of African Women, which has been working patiently and quietly among the deprived for many years. "If you can rise, bring someone with you."

But the advice is generally unheeded, and success is measured as much by one's distance from those below as by one's nearness to those above.

Every possible distinction from the common lot is seized upon and magnified. A person who has been the first to accomplish something automatically acquires status and assumes he is the best. A man who had made a brief trip to the United States as a member of some international sports mission or other never let anyone forget it. For years afterward, whenever he had a chance to speak publicly, he referred to the one fact that differentiated him from his neighbors: "When I was in America...." He had a common name, like Duma, but everyone knew which Duma he was. Throughout the township they called him

Mr. "When-I-Was-in-America" Duma.

Education per se becomes a fetish. People with a college degree may tack it onto their names, signing letters or referring to themselves publicly as "Mr. Soanso, B.A."

All things English are a touchstone. It was under British rule that Africans first believed avenues of advancement were opening for them, and the momentum of these futile hopes is evident in the continuing attraction of English words and English ways.

The ability to speak English is such a distinction that educated Africans may insist on using it in talking to unschooled Africans, who have no idea what is being said.

As far as they are able, middle-class African families will try to behave like Englishmen, copying their dress, their conversational quirks, their mannerisms, and the way they raise their children. The resemblance often is close, except that no amount of posturing can obscure the fact that they are black.

Such people choose their associations with care and move only among Africans they consider to be their equals. The tsotsis contemptuously call them "situations," because they try to reject all but the topmost social situations. They may refuse to sit on a school board because they consider some of the other members beneath them intellectually. Or they may refuse membership in the National Council of African Women because some of those worthy souls are domestic servants. Or, once in an organization, they may prove to have no stomach for hard work; escapism is easier and less troubling. Their township neighbors, irritated by what seems discrimination as senseless as the white's, call them "westernized snobs" and save their admiration for the truly educated.

Perhaps most poignant is the effort to cross the great chasm and make friends with whites. It is possible, though less so every day. A few churchmen, a few liberals, a few fellow members of a few biracial organizations will invite blacks to their homes for tea or tennis or dinner. There is little to be gained, except in terms of status, for the Government is clamping down ever more tightly to prevent interracial contacts. But repression breeds a desperate hunger for identity and approval, and blacks are tempted to accept them from whosoever hand they are offered. In the comfort of a white home, exchanging sprightly and intelligent conversation while sipping tea from a fine china cup, a black man can feel he has escaped the aridity of his township and the monumental dullness of his unlettered neighbors.

Gratitude for being welcomed across the barrier can lead to conviction that the leap has been made not symbolically or experimentally, but on merit, and the pursuit of invitations and the cultivation of white friends may become almost a way of life. Yet by their vulnerability to friendship, Africans may become captivated. They lose sight of the fact of their unalterable blackness and the realities to which this condemns them. By liking and wanting to be liked they may well suffer more than the rejected black who has the distraction and solace of hostility.

False values and muddled objectives have not only confused middle-class Africans socially, but weakened them as a political force and as a source of political leadership. Because of their emotional alliance with whites, they have compromised their own effectiveness. They have clung to the dream of a multiracial society and eagerly accepted the advice and help of white friends. When these have proved undependable, the African's disillusionment has been bitter. But the reality was always there to see. The Government strives for *apartheid*, not togetherness, so that pursuit of the dream has only brought on more repression.

Ultimately, the tragedy of the educated middle-class African is that he offends the Afrikaner's basic image of him as inherently inferior, hence ignorant and submissive, yet withal happy. Anything more than this is cheek, a misguided effort to become an imitation white man. The irony is that every step of the black man's struggle to equip himself for life in a multiracial dream world has alienated the Afrikaner and justified his refusal to grant it. Today there is simply no role for middle-class Africans to play as mediators or peacemakers or exemplars or forerunners in leading the blacks out of bondage. The river is wide and there is no bridge to cross.

Delegates meet at Mamelodi for conference of National Council of African Women.

Left: Old traditions at modern wedding. Women greet couple with symbols of wife's duties to husband and family. Below: Rented car is status symbol at middle-class marriage. Expensive wedding can leave couple broke for a year. Right: Edith Mkhele leads group discussion at African extension of white YWCA. She was first African woman to get degree at white South African college. Below right: Miss Non-White South Africa contest. At microphone is Pete Rezant, director of many social events for Africans. He teaches contestants how to walk, talk, conduct themselves in Western society.

Dr. Mkomo, at NCAW
conference: "We are not a
servant race. We too
have a soul that yearns for
freedom and self-
determination—not development
that is prescribed
and proscribed." Delegates
(below) are women who have
dedicated lives to advancement
of their people.
Opposite: Lillian Ngoyi, member
of since-banned African
National Conference, at meeting
of white liberals.
Middle class sees itself as bridge
between races. Bottom:
Albert Luthuli, president of ANC,
en route to Oslo with
wife to receive Nobel Peace Prize
for 1960. Then—as now—
he was officially in banishment.

BANISHMENT

Banishment is the cruelest and most effective weapon that the South African Government has yet devised to punish its foes and to intimidate potential opposition. Its legal base is a forty-year-old law, the Native Administration Act of 1927. This law empowers the Government, "whenever it is deemed expedient in the general public interest," to move any individual African, or an entire tribe, for that matter, from any place within South Africa to any other place. In effect, this means that any African suspected by the white authorities of being, or thinking about being, a troublemaker can be summarily taken from his home and banished to a remote and desolate detention camp. No prior notice is required. No trial is necessary, no appeal possible, and no time limit set. Banishment can stretch into eternity.

Since 1950, when the current Nationalist administration began implementing the law, some one hundred and forty African men and women have been banished. Most of them once were tribal chiefs, village headmen, or simply men with leadership qualities—in short, influential men whom the Government would wish to neutralize.

What have they done? Where they have been active they have protested or opposed Government policy or a Government-appointed official.

Where they have been inactive, it has been a case of representing a threat that must be removed. In recent years the few remaining tribal areas have reacted against Government policies imposed without consideration of, or consultation with, the people affected. There also has been resistance in the so-called Bantustans, areas set up by the Government as black "homelands." These total 13.7 per cent of the land area of South Africa, but most of it, like American Indian reservations, is arid and unarable, and none of it may be owned by Africans. It is the Government's hope eventually to transfer the entire black population into these enclaves, where they may develop ethnic civilizations independently of the white man and to the limit of their ability.

But the whites give with one hand and take with the other. Since landholding is forbidden to Africans, it is clear that the whites consider even the black homelands still to be theirs, and it follows that they want their own black man keeping an eye on things.

This invariably runs counter to old tribal laws, customs, and usages, and clashes with the authority of hereditary chiefs. To outsiders the Government makes much of the fact that the Bantustans have their own native leaders, but usually they are puppets, with no standing in the

black community. Anyone who protests, however, risks banishment.

Why not jail them, instead? Because even by the arbitrary laws of South Africa there often is no criminal charge that can be brought against them. And, anyway, for a specific crime there is a prescribed punishment. In several years a man would have to be released and could resume his former position in the tribe.

The brilliance of banishment is that it is indeterminate, a limbo which has none of the legal and procedural trappings of prison, yet effectively removes leaders from circulation and breaks up the cohesiveness and forward momentum of the people they left behind.

Perhaps half of those banished over the years have been released—but only after promising the authorities to toe the line. A dozen or so have died in exile. A few have escaped. Today between thirty-five and forty Africans still are in banishment.

The number is small; the enormity is that banishment can happen at all.

Not many people are aware that it does. The only official recognition that the banished even exist is a list of their names posted once a year in the House of Parliament. All I knew about it I had learned from occasional references in the newspapers, but I was determined to visit a banishment camp and see for myself.

The one I picked was Frenchdale, an isolated outpost in the northern reaches of Cape Province, near the border of Botswana, reputedly the worst camp in the system. I made my trip in 1964, driving from Johannesburg in my well-used Volkswagen. My first stop was Mafeking, fifty-six miles away from Frenchdale and still the nearest large town to it.

Here I picked up an acquaintance to help with the car. I wanted to stay in the camp for the better part of a week, but was afraid to have a car with a TJ (Johannesburg) registration hanging about. This is dangerous in outlying areas where whites consider all urban Africans to be cheeky, trouble-making Kaffirs, and are likely to give them a hard time. The acquaintance agreed to drop me off, take the car, and return for me in five days.

We drove for several hours down a dirt road that stretched through miles of flat nothingness. It was arid, semidesert country, treeless and barely able to support scrub. Late at night we reached the banishment camp. At first all I could see was the faint glow of hot coals, the remains of an open cookfire. Then a few black huts took shape, a dozen of them squatting forlornly in a cluster against the long, low skyline. Outside one hut a lone man stood waiting as we approached. We introduced ourselves. He was Piet Mokoena, formerly a tribal leader in the Orange Free State, several hundred miles away, who had been in Frenchdale for ten years.

Soon everybody in the camp came together to greet us. They were so glad to see us, to see anyone. There were six of them—five men and one woman. The youngest was in his thirties. The others were much older. For five days and nights I stayed in Frenchdale with these people. I shared their cookfires and slept in their huts. As I listened to their stories and took the photographs shown here, I got to know something of their feeling of emptiness.

The first thing about the camp that strikes the visitor is the quiet. There were no children's voices, no yipping dogs, none of the murmuring sounds of daily living; there was not even the faraway background hum of passing cars. Nothing. In the sand track we arrived on there was no trace of the tire marks of any other car. I later learned that people who had lived in Mafeking for most of their lives had never heard that there were exiles here.

Shortly after we had been made welcome, my friend departed in the car; the little VW was just too conspicuous. And within a few minutes I began to feel as though I were in banishment myself.

The huts of the banished had dirt floors, concrete walls, and thatch roofs. There were no lavatories or baths, and no electricity. The only light was the feeble glow of a tiny paraffin lamp with a wick of string. The nearest water was three-quarters of a mile away, and early each evening, as coolness crept over the land, a trek was made to fill the water cans for the next day.

Food was a problem. There never was enough. The Government says coolly that banishment is

not legal incarceration, like jail, and that therefore it is under no obligation to feed or clothe or equip the banished. In recent years it has allotted each of the banished four rand ($5.60) per month, three in meal and one in cash which goes to purchase extras. This comes not as a right, but as a favor. Once each month the group hikes twelve miles to a village to receive their grants and to spend them at the one store there. Then they hike home again. It is an ordeal for these aging people, but it is also the big event of their month.

One of the men owned a pressure cooker. The others prepared their meals over open fires, brewing a porridge that grew thinner as the month progressed. Occasionally there were gifts of food or milk from compassionate Africans living in the vicinity. The several sacks of flour and maize meal I had brought along were gratefully accepted; on the way to Frenchdale they also had served as hiding places for my cameras (each in its plastic bag) in case the police should become curious and stop me.

Aside from a few goats and chickens, the people of Frenchdale grew none of their own food. "If only we had hoes or shovels," Piet Mokoena told me, "any tools at all to farm with, we could start a garden and try to make something grow in this sand." One day while I was there three tiny chicks turned up on the roasting fire: They had frozen to death the night before.

Piet Mokoena, I learned, had once had a chance to leave Frenchdale. The authorities had offered to let him go home if he promised never again to say or do anything against the Government. Stubbornly, he refused. "At the time you took me away from my home," he told them, "you said my people had told you I was bad. Now you have had me for ten years. Am I no longer bad? And if so, how did that bad turn to good?"

Piet's hut was immaculately clean, a sign that he had not yet entirely given up. Except for one old chair there was no furniture. No bed. He slept on goatskins, the contribution of animals he had raised himself. Here he spent his days in meditation.

Paulus Mopeli, a Basotho chief and grandson of the great leader, Moshesh, had been in Frenchdale for fourteen years. Fortunately, after three years in banishment he had been reunited with his wife, Treaty, when she too was banished. At the time of my visit, she was sixty-six and the only woman in the camp. Her face was as worn and wrinkled as her tattered hat, and she still worried over the fate of a six-year-old grandchild who had been pushed out by the police and told to fend for himself the night Treaty was picked up.

The chief refused on principle to accept his meager monthly grant from the Government. He got by on small gifts mailed from home and on help from the others. His crime had been to refuse to cull his herd. The Government tries to reduce the headcount of native cattle because it says there are more animals than the land will support. But the tribesmen often resist, saying that it is not a matter of too many animals, but of too little land. Owning cattle is of great importance to them; a good herd makes the tribe independent. So, the Government first gets the leading resisters—like Chief Paulus—out of the way and then culls the herd.

The chief would not allow me to photograph him. "I've been in banishment too long. Nothing will free me. All I'm waiting for is death."

Still another man, Alex Tekane, did not know what crime he had been banished for. He remembered that he and a friend had been accused of insulting a Government-installed chief and had been fined £25 ($70) apiece. They had appealed and won, and the next thing he knew the police were at his home reading a banishment order to him in English, which he does not understand. He was put on a train, under escort, and delivered to Frenchdale. After five years of banishment he was still sitting there, wondering why.

Theophilus Tshangela is tired and sickly. He spends much of his time lying on an old jute mattress stuffed with grass and reading his Bible. With an old man's finickiness he has arranged his clothes on wire hooks around the walls of his hut. Is there no doctor for him? Yes, there is a district surgeon, but he turns up in his own good time. Even then he does not stay long. He rarely examines anyone, just says, "Here is some medicine. Take it." The patients have no idea what is being prescribed and fear that it may

harm more than help; often they throw it away.

The banished ones told me that some time back they had had a young wife in the camp who realized that she was going to give birth prematurely. Her husband walked the twelve miles to the village in order to call the district surgeon, and he promised to come. Several days later he did. By that time 'the woman had undergone a premature delivery unattended. For a while, at least, Frenchdale heard the lively sound of a baby crying.

Only one man held tightly to his hopes for the future. This was Leonford Ganyile, the youngest of the group. He continued steadfastly to study for his matriculation with texts sent to him by friends and sympathizers on the outside. Long afterward I heard that he had escaped from Frenchdale.

Not surprisingly, a few of the banished had lost count of the days. Monday looks like Friday in Frenchdale. Nothing breaks the monotony. Nothing breaks the unvarying routine. There are no youngsters at home on Saturday, no church bells on Sunday, no rush and hurry of shopping days and laundry days during the week. What is Christmas like? Like every other day. Only sunrise and sunset marked the days. The passage from light to darkness was their calendar.

Most men, I learned, refused to allow their wives and children to accompany them into banishment. Paulus was the exception; but he and Treaty were old and a comfort to each other in their declining years. For younger people, the choice was clear. With no schools available and no employment, there would be no sense in imprisoning one's family, as well. If a man was lucky, he might be visited once or twice a year by his family, despite the one bus from Mafeking to the village and the hard, twelve-mile walk to the camp.

Some families, of course, do not know where their husband and father has gone. The police have no obligation to inform a man where he is being taken, none to tell his wife and children where they can find him. Paulus Mopeli was separated from Treaty for years because she, too, was banished while he was being detained, first in jail and then at Uitkyk, a tribal area in the bush. It was only by accident that Treaty was also sent there and that they were transferred to Frenchdale together.

Aside from rare and bittersweet visits from relatives, the banished are almost entirely cut off from society. The Government's lack of interest is profound. There have been cases when the officials in charge have not known whether a man had been released or was still vegetating in a camp.

Drowning in dullness, the once-keen intellects of the banished rehash old grievances, engage in old arguments. Precious letters from home are read over and over again. Letters are saved for years until they yellow and crumble.

One day during my stay brought excitement into the life of the camp and would be remembered more vividly than the rest. This was when the police van from the village came to call. We had plenty of warning. The dust it stirred up could be seen from a distance. I went out and hid in the bush, the endless bush surrounding the camp. Whatever else might have been wrong, I was an unauthorized visitor and had no right to be there. Actually, as I later learned, they had seen the tracks of my Volkswagen. They knew that the road to the camp was almost never used and had become suspicious. The banished ones were most unhelpful. They fell silent, staring at the police with vacant and listless eye. They had little to fear from their noncooperation. There was nothing the police could do; the banished already were at the end of the line. Eventually, when the police could find no trace of my car or me, and could elicit no answers to their questions, they went away. A plume of dust trailed their car back down the track. The sound of its motor dwindled away. Soon the customary silence settled over the camp, and the banished idled away the remaining hours till evening fell.

For them an infinity of unremarkable days stretched ahead. For me the frightful nothingness of Frenchdale was about to end. In another day or so my friend came back for me in the Volkswagen, as we had arranged, and after saying our good-byes we drove away. We reached home without incident. Ironically, as I reentered the restricted black life of Johannesburg I felt free.

Frenchdale banishment camp: twelve huts with nothing around them but miles of barren veld

The six Africans living
in Frenchdale are completely
cut off from the world.
Seen through the doorway
of one man's hut is
his never-changing view of
neighboring huts
and sunbaked veldt.

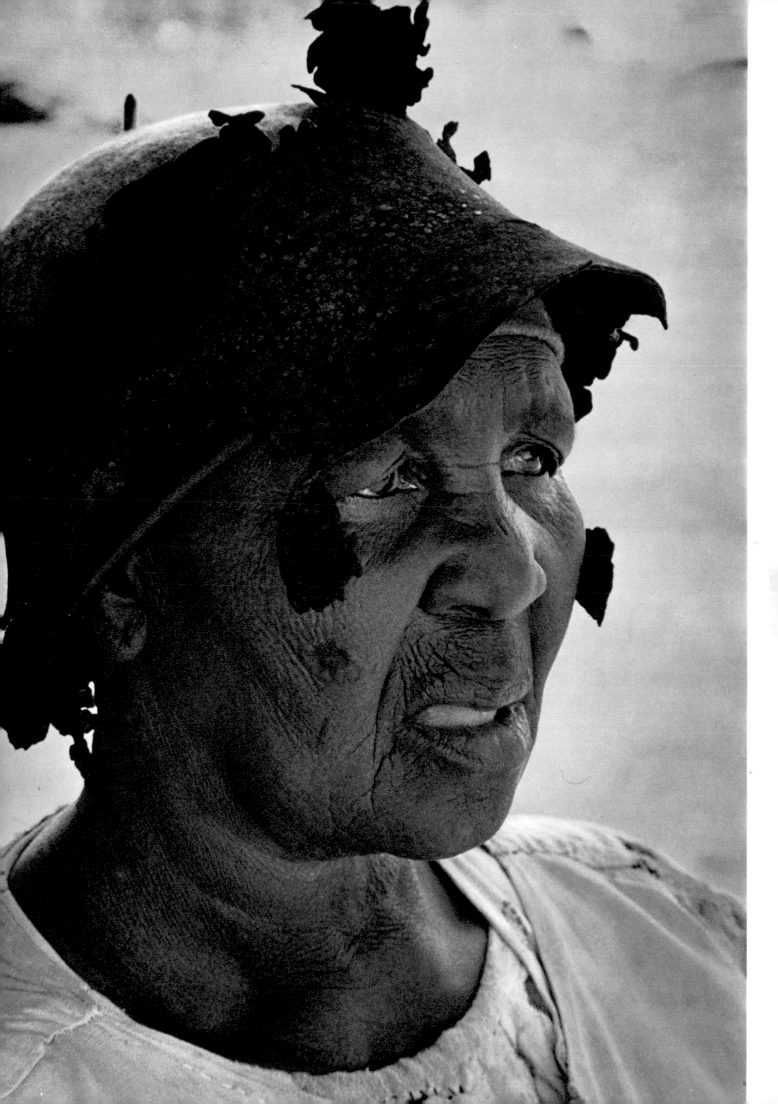

Treaty Mopeli's face and hat are battered by years of banishment. She still worries about a grandchild made homeless the night she was taken by police. Her husband Paulus (below), once a Basotho chief, was banished in 1950. Above: chicks that died from night cold roast on Treaty's stove.

Water from a borehole three-quarters
of a mile away is fetched in early morning
and evening, when sun has lost
its sting. Frenchdale is in semidesert area,
very hot during day, very cold
at night. At the end of a day there is
nothing to do but sleep. Far right:
Leonford Ganyile was hopeful for future and
studied for his matriculation by
the light of a paraffin lamp. He later
escaped across Botswana border.

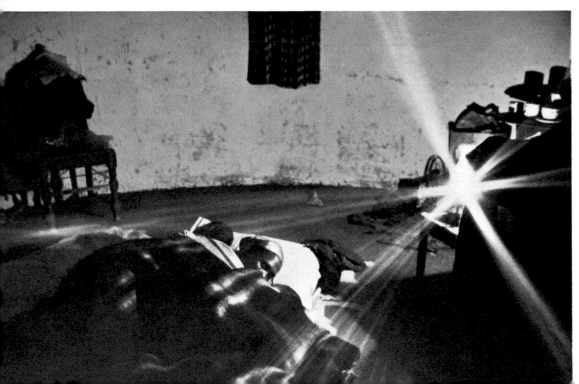

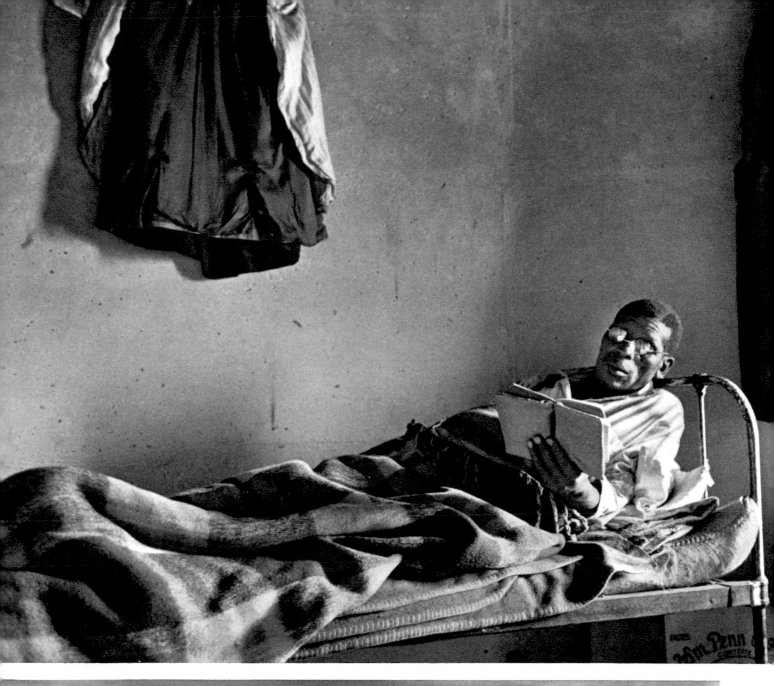

Theophilus Tshangela (above) lies alone in his sickness and reads his prayer book. His mattress is jute bag filled with grass. Left: Little news filters in from outside, and conversation on the same old topics sometimes flares with irritation. Right: Piet Mokoena spends hours meditating, reading and rereading old letters and the Bible.

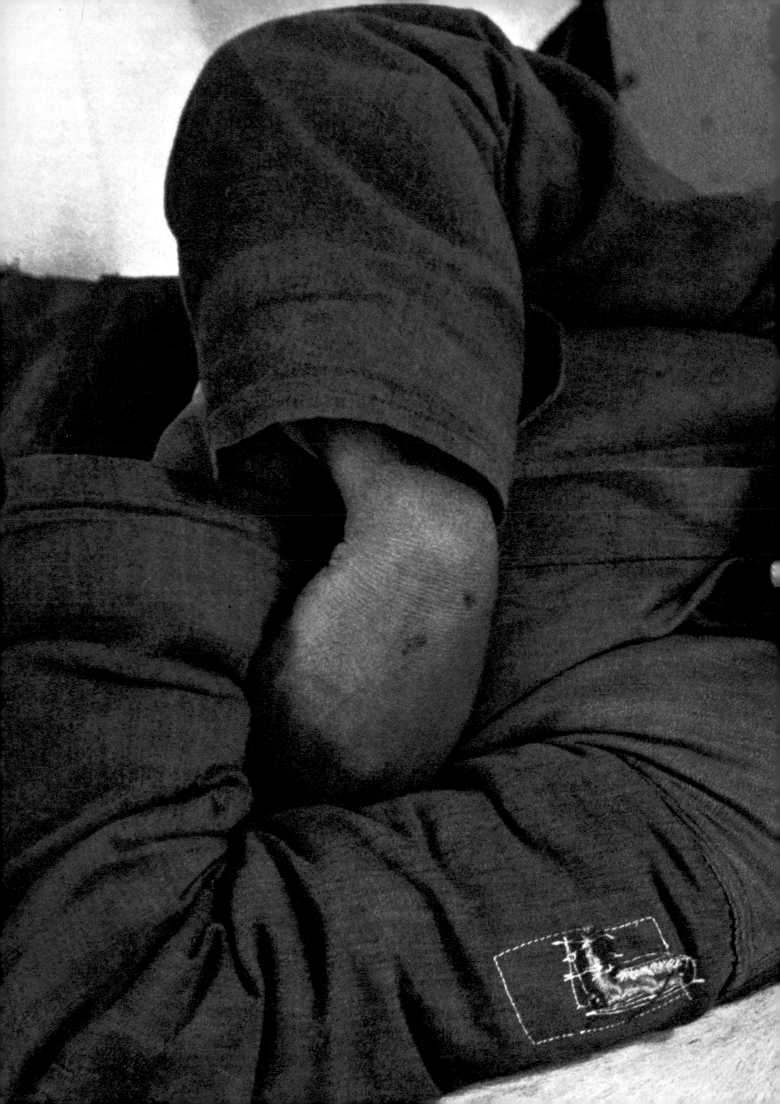

Piet falls asleep with Bible on his face. Africans say: "When the Europeans came, they had the Bible and we had the land. Now we have the Bible, and they have our land."

About Ernest Cole

Ernest Cole is a member of the Bapedi, a subgroup of three major tribes making up the black population of South Africa—and he must be the most traveled twenty-seven-year-old member the tribe has ever had. Ernest is strictly an urban person, a product of an industrial system that has conscripted his people as a labor force but has refused to assimilate them as human beings. For this book he spent more than five years photographing life in South Africa as it looks from the wrong side of the color line.

Ernest was born March 21, 1940, in his family's six-room brick house in Eersterust, a black township ten miles outside Pretoria, South Africa's administrative capital. He was the fourth of six children. His mother was (and is) a washerwoman who does laundry for white families in Pretoria. Ernest's father, who was born in the tribal village but left home as a young man and never went back, worked at home as a tailor, altering coats and mending clothes for African customers.

Although the family lived from hand to mouth, it was not desperately poor by African standards. Nevertheless, food was scarce and Ernest nearly died of malnutrition when he was three months old. Now at his full growth he stands five feet four inches and weighs just over one hundred pounds.

Ernest was a quick student in the all-black schools he attended, and he yearned to become a doctor. But encroaching *apartheid* cut that dream short. Ernest's class in secondary school was the first to have its certificates stamped "Bantu Education" in the then-new Government program to limit the education of Africans. Ernest's angry response was to quit school at sixteen and undertake to finish his course by correspondence.

Ernest spent most of his first year out of school looking for a job. Although South Africa was booming, the opportunities for a dark-skinned teen-ager were limited. He worked variously as a clerk, a messenger, and for one stretch as an assistant to a Chinese studio photographer, who paid him little but gave him his first professional equipment: a Yashica C with flash attachment. Eventually, Ernest caught on with *Zonk*, a now-defunct magazine for Africans, as a combination tea maker, office duster, bill collector, and subscription salesman, but not as a photographer.

His first real professional opportunities came in 1958 from Jurgen Schaderberg, picture editor of *Drum* magazine. He enrolled in a correspondence course offered by the New York Institute of Photography, whose ad he had seen in an American magazine. Within a year, he felt encouraged enough to settle on photojournalism as his vocation—and a book about South African life as his special project. In 1965, Ernest decided to work full-time to complete the book. A year later he had his pictures, but at the last moment nearly lost both them and his freedom.

While photographing pass arrests, he was picked up for interrogation. Twice before he had explained away his picture-taking with nimble answers to hectoring police. But this time he knew that even a casual search would uncover his many years of work and that his files would be seized.

Once again, however, Ernest was saved by his wits. He explained that his pass-arrest pictures were for a story on juvenile delinquency among Africans. The police were impressed and offered him an opportunity to be an informer. Ernest said he would think it over. After he was allowed to go he decided it was time to leave the country.

He managed to get a passport by joining, for the moment, a group of pilgrims to Lourdes. He departed South Africa by plane one step ahead of the law, and has journeyed since to London, Paris, and New York.

"You've won your ten carrots, anyway," Max reminded him.

"That's all right. You can keep the carrots," said Coriander.

"Great," said Joe, who loved carrots. "Let's play tag then. You're it."

The three little rabbits sat in the glade once again. "We thought the fox had got you," said Joe, when Coriander had finished telling them about his adventure.

"*Is* there such a thing as an Easter bunny?" asked Max.

"I'm sure there is," said Coriander thoughtfully. "The humans certainly think there is, especially the little humans and I like them best." He was thinking of Anna. He hoped she would get lots of Easter eggs. "But I know one thing now," he said. "You can't *become* an Easter bunny. You either are one or you're not. And I'm not."

"Can't we keep him?" asked Anna, when they arrived at the edge of the forest.

"No, my dear," said her father. "Rabbits belong in the forests and fields. You know that!"

"Suppose he really *is* the Easter bunny?" she said.

"Then he will bring you a special treat tomorrow," said Father.

"There's no such thing as an Easter bunny," said Stephen.

Anna took the little rabbit out of the basket and gently set him down on the grass. As Coriander hopped away he just heard her whisper: "I know you really are the Easter bunny."

Anna, Stephen and their father sat in the back seat of the car. Anna had the basket on her lap. Coriander was curled up inside, not feeling at all well. He hated the shaking and rattling, and the noise of the car's engine. Suddenly a child's hand came into the basket, and Coriander felt someone gently stroking him. He was much less frightened now.

At last Mr. Smith gave in. He rang the forester and asked him to return the little rabbit to freedom.

"Rabbits don't belong in shop windows," said the forester, as he put Coriander carefully into a basket.

"Especially Easter bunnies!" said Anna indignantly.

"I don't understand it," grumbled the shopkeeper. "He seemed so happy at first...."

The first people to notice he wasn't happy were Anna and Stephen. Then the other children saw it, and soon even the grown-ups knew that Mr. Smith's Easter bunny was homesick.

An angry crowd gathered in the street, shouting at Mr. Smith and telling him to take the poor creature back to the forest. No one would buy anything from the shop as long as the little rabbit remained in the window.

By the fourth day Coriander didn't even want to look at a carrot. He wasn't hopping around anymore and he'd stopped trying to paint eggs. He just lay on the artificial grass, remembering his own little forest glade and wishing he was back there. He'd had quite enough of being an Easter bunny.

And while the children pressed their noses against the shop window, the grown-ups were spending money in Mr. Smith's shop. They bought plain eggs, decorated eggs, eggs made of chocolate, marzipan and sugar, and chocolate bunnies in all shapes and sizes. The most popular item of all was an Easter cake with a marzipan model of Coriander on the top.

Every evening Mr. Smith brought the little rabbit a huge carrot. But, though the carrots got bigger and juicier every day, Coriander was beginning to lose his appetite.

Mr. Smith stood outside his shop feeling very pleased with himself. His Easter bunny workshop looked splendid. And there in the middle of it, hopping around with a paintbrush in his paw, was Coriander.

Soon the whole village was talking about the Easter bunny's workshop. People came from far and wide to see the bunny at work.

Coriander was so busy that he didn't even know he was in danger until the jacket landed on him and everything went black. "Got you, Easter bunny!" said a voice, close to his ear.

Coriander was only frightened for a moment. "If he thinks I'm an Easter bunny I'm quite safe," he thought. "People don't hurt Easter bunnies."

Coriander was at the edge of the wood licking flower petals and trying to stick them on an egg. He knew that Easter bunnies decorated eggs and he was determined to learn how to do it.

He didn't realize that he was being watched. Albert Smith, the owner of the biggest grocery store in the village, was staring at the little rabbit and rubbing his hands together. "Just what I need," he muttered. He imagined his shop window as an Easter bunny's workshop, with a real, live rabbit working there. It would be a sensation. What a lot of money he could make! He took off his jacket and crept up behind Coriander.

There were once three little rabbits sitting in a forest glade, not peacefully nibbling the grass as you might expect, but shouting at each other. "You can't be an Easter bunny," yelled Max, the clever one. "There's no such thing."

"If you were an Easter bunny you'd have to go near humans and humans are terribly dangerous," said Joe, the timid one.

"I *can* be an Easter bunny," said Coriander, the smallest of the three. "I bet you, if I were an Easter bunny the humans wouldn't hurt me. Yes, I bet you ten carrots!"

Coriander's Easter Adventure

BY **Ingrid Ostheeren**

ILLUSTRATED BY

Jean-Pierre Corderoc'h

TRANSLATED BY

ROSEMARY LANNING

North-South Books

NEW YORK

For Uli

Copyright © 1992 by Nord-Süd Verlag AG, Gossau Zürich, Switzerland
First published in Switzerland under the title *Coriander wird Osterhase*
English translation copyright © 1992 by Rosemary Lanning

First published in the United States, Great Britain, Canada,
Australia and New Zealand in 1992 by North-South Books,
an imprint of Nord-Süd Verlag AG, Gossau Zürich, Switzerland.

Distributed in the United States by North-South Books Inc., New York.

Library of Congress Cataloging-in-Publication Data
Ostheeren, Ingrid.
[Coriander wird Osterhase. English]
Coriander's Easter adventure / by Ingrid Ostheeren; illustrated
by Jean-Pierre Corderoc'h; translated by Rosemary Lanning.
Summary: When Coriander, a little rabbit, expresses a desire to be
an Easter bunny, he has an unexpected adventure.
ISBN 1-55858-136-7 (trade)
ISBN 1-5585-150-2 (lib. bdg.)
[1. Easter—Fiction. 2. Rabbits—Fiction.] I. Corderoc'h,
Jean-Pierre, ill. II. Title.
PZ7.0847Co 1992
[E]—dc20 91-26867

British Library Cataloguing in Publication Data
Ostheeren, Ingrid
Coriander's Easter adventure.
I. Title II. [Coriander wird Osterhase. *English*]
833.914 [J]

ISBN 1-55858-136-7

1 3 5 7 9 10 8 6 4 2
Printed in Belgium